KEEP YOUR ENEMIES CLOSER

KEEP YOUR ENEMIES CLOSER

ALISON BROWNSTONE™ BOOK ELEVEN

JUDITH BERENS   MARTHA CARR   MICHAEL ANDERLE

LMBPN

DISRUPTIVE IMAGINATION®

Copyright © 2019 Judith Berens, Martha Carr and Michael Anderle
Cover by Fantasy Book Design
Cover copyright © LMBPN Publishing
A Michael Anderle Production

LMBPN Publishing
PMB 196, 2540 South Maryland Pkwy
Las Vegas, NV 89109

First US edition, July 2019
Print ISBN: 978-1-64202-382-4

Thanks to the JIT Readers

Dave Hicks
Diane L. Smith
John Ashmore
Nicole Emens
Shari Regan
Daniel Weigert
Peter Manis
Jeff Eaton
Paul Westman
Peter Manis
Dorothy Lloyd
Misty Roa

If we've missed anyone, please let us know!

Editor
SkyHunter Editing Team

DEDICATIONS

From Martha

To everyone who still believes in magic
and all the possibilities that holds.
To all the readers who make this
entire ride so much fun.
And to my son, Louie and so many wonderful friends who
remind me all the time of what
really matters and how wonderful
life can be in any given moment.

From Michael

To Family, Friends and
Those Who Love
To Read.
May We All Enjoy Grace
To Live The Life We Are
Called.

CHAPTER ONE

An explosive shockwave pounded into Alison and knocked her off her feet. Her shield could only do so much when she didn't have both feet planted firmly on the ground. Trunks shattered around her and fir trees toppled like pins scattered by a bowling ball but with extended splintering groans. She pushed onto her feet. Her wounds stung, but her layered shields had saved her life. She summoned another protective barrier and extended a new shadow blade.

Yeah, Mason was right about this plan.

"Tahir, what's the progress of the other team?" she asked. "I'm taking serious firepower here."

There was no response.

She patted her ear and scowled. "Damn." Her receiver was gone, no doubt dislodged by the last attack. Something whistled ominously as it rocketed toward her.

Here we go again.

Alison extended shadow wings and launched upward a second before a pulsating orb struck the ground a few yards away. The latest blast and shockwave hurled her unceremoniously into a thick tree trunk. She slid down it with a grunt and tried to drag in a breath to replace the air the impact had forced from her lungs.

"I'll handle distracting the cannon!" That sounded so cool when I said it, but Drysi, Hana, and Mason had better hurry before the smugglers blow most of the forest away. How would we explain that?

Sorry, folks, the Olympic National Forest burned down because Alison Brownstone is incompetent.

She released her wings and flung a shadow line out, pulled herself to a new tree, and immediately directed another line to continue the process. Her new movement kept her in motion but the cannon fire continued relentlessly. The ordnance struck the trees behind her and created new clearings.

The actual job, in theory, was supposed to be simple. Agent Latherby had trouble obtaining permission for a raid against a group of wizard arms smugglers. His PDA superiors wanted to wait longer and collect more evidence before apprehending them. They believed they could catch a few bigger fish that way, but when he'd learned the smugglers had brought over a gnome-created explosive cannon that didn't even require magic to fire, the agent had appealed to a few supervisors. Fortunately, they agreed with him. Unfortunately, they couldn't gather the necessary resources in time due to bureaucracy. So Latherby reached out to Alison and gave her a straightforward mission—destroy the cannon and secure the smugglers.

As the weapon possessed homing capabilities, approaching the wizards directly would end with the

2

Brownstone Team blown to pieces. She had decided to distract the enemy while her team negotiated their magical trap-laden forest compound and surprised the smugglers.

I can do this. I only need to keep stalling. The cannon has to run out of power eventually.

Another onslaught leveled a half-dozen trees. Alison changed course and attempted to make her way back toward the wizards' compound. Eventually had never seemed so far away.

This is not my favorite day.

She summoned new wings and thrust herself upward before she leveled off several yards from the treetops. If she lost her cover, the gnome cannon would eliminate her with ease. Then again, if she remained too close to the ground, the explosions would most likely be able to do the same thing. She spun and dodged a blast. It curved but struck a tree and obliterated the top, and flaming debris erupted to shower the area.

Good thing it's wet and February. If I could only catch my breath, I could counterattack with a blast of my own.

Alison dove to avoid another missile. The pulsating glob of energy looped toward her. She looked over her shoulder before she thrust toward a nearby tree. A quick twist at the last moment helped her dodge the trunk but the trailing attack decimated it. She pushed forward through a cloud of fire, wood dust, and smoke.

I wish Latherby had known a little more about the cannon.

Over the next minute or two, she remained on the move and changed course erratically. As she spun and twisted, all while randomly altering her altitude, she realized something very important.

Wait a second. They stopped firing. Did they finally run out of power or did the team reach the cannon?

She exhaled a sigh of relief, turned toward the wizard compound, and accelerated. Smoke poured from the forest in the distance to identify her target. She lowered her altitude to skim along the ground and eased to a stop only a few yards away from the building.

Here we go.

From the outside, the facility appeared to be nothing more than a hill covered with fallen logs, but her careful eye identified the runes and wards carved into trees and rocks in the area. The smoke that had guided her poured from a jagged hole in the side of the faux hill. Several logs smoldered nearby. A few wizards in camouflaged fatigues rushed out, their wands in hand, thoroughly distracted as they coughed and wheezed for clean air. She disabled them with rapid stun bolts before they even realized they were under attack.

So the cannon didn't run out of power. Good job, guys.

Alison jogged closer to the hole and extended a shadow blade. She created a light orb and an air bubble as she entered the darkened tunnel. Several bodies sprawled in the entrance. Some had stopped breathing, while others groaned, half-conscious. Although their orders didn't call for explicit neutralization, Agent Latherby made it clear he didn't expect the Brownstone Team to not defend themselves.

A scream in the distance spurred her into action and she sprinted toward the source. Thirty seconds later, she arrived in a sprawling artificial cavern filled with dozens of crates and tables with artifacts of various types on display

—everything from glowing swords to a silver pipe that radiated intense magic. A huge rune-covered golden cannon lay on its side in a circle of burning debris, the main cause of the smoke.

How did they even fire that thing out of here?

She shook her head. The mysteries of powerful gnome artifacts could wait. If the PDA had their way, they would lock the damned thing up in a warehouse where no one would ever find it. It wouldn't be her problem, then, and not soon enough, either. She was over this.

More wizards lay on the ground and most were wounded but alive. Drysi stood with a knife held to the throat of a wide-eyed wizard and smiled. Hana's tails were fully on display as she wiped her bloodied claws on her shirt. Mason moved from one man to the next and confiscated their wands. There was no reason to let anyone surprise them.

He looked at her, relief on his face. "You had me worried, A, when we lost comms with you." He glared at the wizards. "I don't know what I would have done if these bastards had hurt you."

Alison shrugged and pointed to a scratch. "I haven't had time to heal, but it wasn't so bad. Even with their fancy homing capability, they had trouble landing a direct hit. I'm not saying I wouldn't have preferred if you guys had stopped them earlier." She gestured to the toppled cannon. "You blasted it directly, huh?"

Drysi grinned and forced the wizard to his knees before she snapped a zip-tie on him. "The PDA said we had to stop them from selling it, but they didn't say anything about keeping it one piece. Still, it's held up fairly well."

"Yeah, too bad it's not slag." She nodded. Fewer dangerous artifacts in the world wouldn't hurt. "Did you guys catch the leader? Technically, these guys have an organizational bounty, and he has a bounty as well, so that's a nice bonus I can spread around."

Hana gestured to a bearded man with a chest laceration who lay with his back against a crate.

Alison marched over to him. "I'm sorry, but if I thought I could have persuaded you to surrender, we wouldn't have done something like this. Everything we were told said you'd fight no matter how we approached you."

"We have pride." The man grunted and his face twisted in pain. "But you're nothing but a government lapdog. You were lucky this time."

She rolled her eyes. "Lapdog? But guess what? I don't care." She gestured at their surroundings. "Because I don't think you had grand plans to save the world or help those who are oppressed. I know all about the kind of people you help—terrorists and organized crime—and you also help your bank account."

The wizard hocked a bloody glob of spit at her feet. "Screw you, Brownstone. You've made a powerful enemy today. I hope you realize that."

"Made a powerful enemy?" She shrugged. "That's like every week for me. It's a job hazard. I'll have my assistant pen you in for a vicious final battle, but you'll have to get in line. For now, you have a date with the PDA."

CHAPTER TWO

There were certain sentences a woman didn't expect to hear when running a security company. Ava had offered a number of them in the last few minutes of discussion at the conference room table, and she was ready to add more. Several days had passed since they had raided the arms smugglers' camp, and other issues had become more pressing at the Brownstone Building.

"The Kingdom of Fur and Snuggles," Ava explained in a smooth voice as she looked at her tablet, "is willing to offer a significant discount if we agree to purchase a year's worth of their products in one transaction. We have significant unused storage in the building, so that wouldn't be an issue if you decide we should take them up on it."

I wonder what the underworld would think if they knew I was buying from a place called the Kingdom of Fur and Snuggles. The Dark Princess wuvs her little fur babykins.

Alison scrubbed a hand down her face. "This pet park is getting expensive for something we only use as cover for

Omni. Sometimes, I think we should simply hide him in a tunnel or something."

Her assistant pushed her glasses up her nose. "Please consider, Miss Brownstone, the potential dual uses of the pet park. It might prove unexpectedly useful for improving the morale of the non-magical field teams."

"Yeah. I've already heard considerable positive feedback from employees about it." She sighed. "It doesn't matter. Until we know the Tapestry's finished, we need to keep Omni in a safe place where we can keep an eye on him. At the same time, I don't want people to build up too much of a complex about special treatment for Hana or where and when they can bring pets to work." She considered all the logistics. "I hope we can eventually tell the rest of the company. I don't like having to keep this from them, but too many questions remain. They don't need to worry about that kind of thing. It's obvious the Tapestry isn't willing to attack the Brownstone Building."

"Of course, Miss Brownstone. Do you have any additional information on how to handle the Tapestry?"

She shook her head. "I have a few ideas, but they'll require me to bring in outside people. It also means I need to bring the core team up to speed on a few details." She gestured to a clock on the wall. "It's almost time for our meeting anyway."

Ava nodded, a knowing look in her eyes. Alison didn't know if the woman knew what she was about to explain but she wouldn't be at all surprised if she did.

The door opened and Hana stepped inside, followed by Tahir, Drysi, and Mason. She waited for her team to take a seat, stood, and closed the door before she returned to her place at the front of the table and raised her hands. After a deep breath, she slowly extended a bubble of silence around them with the help of a quick incantation.

Mason raised an eyebrow. "What are you doing, A?" He looked around the room.

"We have many wards on this building, but I want to be extra careful. I'm simply making sure we have complete privacy, as this will be an unusual conversation, even by our standards." She looked around the table at each of her friends and employees. "What I'm about to say doesn't leave this room. That includes Sonya. I'm not saying that because I don't trust her. I'm saying that for her own protection."

Tahir nodded.

Hana wrinkled her nose. "That sounds creepy. What's up?"

"I called this meeting because we need to talk about Omni," she explained.

The fox shrugged. "It's been a month, and he hasn't gone into Angry Omni mode, even when a stupid poodle growled at him the other day. I think he's more than proven he's stable." She huffed her annoyance.

Drysi chuckled. "Plenty of people have pets that don't get angry until someone threatens their owner. My cousin had this bloody lazy Corgi who wouldn't do anything but lay around. He let anyone pet him and little children could tug on his fur. One day, my cousin went out for a walk, and this bastard decided to mug him. He punched my cousin— a right painful hit too. The Corgi turned feral. It practically ripped the other man's throat out. The criminal ended up in the hospital for two weeks."

Mason grimaced. "What did your cousin do?"

"Gave the Corgi his own room." The Welsh witch shrugged.

Hana nodded. "Good doggie." She turned to Alison. "Are you worried about Omni hurting someone?"

"No, not at this point, unless they're Tapestry." She frowned and persevered. "It's more that we need to discover what he is so we can identify who and what the Tapestry are. And I think, to do that, we need to expand the range of possibilities."

Tahir looked confused. "Meaning what?"

Okay, here we go.

Alison took a deep breath. "There's something I've been wanting to tell you all for a while, but it wasn't my secret to tell. I've talked to my dad and mom about it, and they've both given me the go-ahead."

"Tell us what, A?" Mason asked, his tone tinged with concern.

"My father is an alien," she said quietly.

Tahir narrowed his eyes. "You're talking about your adopted father, James Brownstone?"

She nodded. "Yeah."

Drysi shrugged. "So, he's Oriceran? What's the big deal? I always thought the idea he was merely a human with special magical armor didn't sound right. He can do amazing things without it, too. I simply assumed it enhanced his power."

Alison shook her head. "No, you don't understand. Dad's not an Oriceran, he's an alien. He was born on a different planet in this galaxy to a race called the Vax. His parents sent him here as a baby because they didn't want him to be forced into being a super-soldier for their violent, genocidal government. That armor he has isn't merely armor. It's an advanced biotechnological symbiont, and it's intelligent."

Hana blinked several times. "Whoa. I mean…whoa."

Ava set her tablet down and folded her hands. Some notes shouldn't exist, and a good assistant understood that even when the notes were kept secure.

Drysi laughed. "What? Being a half-Drow princess wasn't good enough for you? You had to go and have a Martian dad, too?"

Alison chuckled.

Mason stared at her. "That's…" He shook his head. "But I thought all stories about aliens were only mistaken identity cases with Oricerans. No one even talks about contacting other planets anymore with the gates open."

"Many of the stories are mistaken identity. Maybe even most." She shrugged. "But there are numerous planets out there with intelligent life, and most of them are way more advanced technologically than Earth. There's a kind of UN for at least some of them called the Nine Systems Alliance. They're watching Earth. They're leery of my dad because to them, the Vax are these scary, conquering aliens, and they are right about most of them. Remember that Broken Wand incident in LA?"

Tahir scoffed. "I knew it. I've been convinced for years it was some kind of invasion that was covered up, but I couldn't figure out who. I'd assumed it was some rogue faction from Oriceran and the government didn't want to raise tensions."

Alison shook her head. "A small group of Vax invaded,

and the Nine Systems Alliance intended to bombard LA to stop them. My dad stopped the Vax, and the government stopped the Alliance in space."

Drysi whistled. "This is bloody crazy, but I don't get why this is all a secret. I'm a witch in a room with a Drow, wizards, and a nine-tailed fox. Spacemen seem almost normal."

"She said it herself," Tahir reminded her. "They're technologically advanced. It might be that we have little ability to counter them if they attacked in force. If they have FTL travel, it also means they probably have ships capable of destroying Earth with ease. If people knew about that, they'd panic, and it'd destabilize everything between Earth and Oriceran. Which isn't all that stable, to begin with, of course."

Alison nodded. "Tahir's right. Earth and Oriceran do have one big advantage, though. The Nine Systems Alliance and the Vax don't have magic. You were all around Dad in Vancouver. Did any of you notice that Hana didn't sense magic from him?"

Mason frowned. "Damn. There was so much going on, I didn't notice."

Hana wrinkled her nose. "Me neither."

The infomancer looked at Alison and understanding dawned in his eyes. "Do you think Omni or the Tapestry might be aliens?"

"It's a possibility," she suggested. "The Alliance acts like there isn't magic anywhere else in the galaxy except on Earth and Oriceran, so that suggests it's at least rare. They've mentioned psionic powers that are kind of like magic, but we clearly sense magic from Omni and the Tapestry, even if it's strange."

Mason frowned. "Then they might simply be weird Oricerans and have nothing to do with aliens."

"That's true, but I wanted to lay all my cards on the table. The more possibilities we accept, the better we'll be able to look for evidence."

Ava cleared her throat. "Might I suggest another possibility, Miss Brownstone?"

Everyone turned to focus on the English administrative assistant and waited.

"There are very few civilizations that are comfortable having an obvious weakness." The woman gestured to the tablet. "On our planet, for much of the past ten thousand years, closing the technological gap has been the most important issue. Now, closing the magical gap is, but it's not incredibly difficult to conceptualize given that we still had magicals here, even when the gates were closed." A slight frown marred her face. "You've already seen what happens when someone worries about the implications of not having a tool an enemy might possess."

"I'm not following you, Ava," Alison admitted.

"Scott Carlyle spent his money and time on experiments, whether it was technomagic or his biological efforts. He lacked magic, and in his view, non-magical civilization was something separate."

Tahir furrowed his brow in thought. "You're saying the Tapestry might be aliens performing magical experiments?"

Ava shrugged. "I'm merely presenting it as one possibility. Omni might be some kind of experimental subject."

Hana snorted. "I don't like animal testing when humans do it, and I won't let it go for evil alien freaks."

"We don't know." Alison frowned. "We need to capture a Tapestry member and interrogate them. The way their bodies disintegrate, we can't do much with dead ones."

Mason sighed. "I'm not saying I disagree, but if they really are aliens, shouldn't we involve the government in this? We can't take on an alien invasion ourselves."

"Maybe. I do have contacts in the government who are aware of aliens and are part of anti-alien efforts, but I want to step lightly in this. We don't know that they are aliens, and I don't want them to come and try to lock Omni up." She grimaced. "My dad's had a lot of...unpleasant dealings with the government over alien stuff. To this day, they're watching him, and the less we can involve them, the better."

Tahir nodded. "I agree, but there might come a point where we have no choice."

"For now, there's not much we can do," Alison replied, frustration etched on her face. "Unless you've found some evidence?"

He shook his head. "I've scoured for unusual activity that might be associated with them, along with keeping extra drone watch on our respective homes and the Brownstone Building, and I've found nothing to indicate they're close to us."

Drysi snorted. "They had a right proper beating the last time. They might not be eager to challenge us again."

"That's true." Alison nodded. "But they obviously need or want Omni for some reason, and given the way they acted, it definitely won't be good."

"What if it really is an alien invasion?" Hana asked, her eyes wide.

"An invasion with a handful of guys?" Mason countered. "Yes, they had a decent number of soldiers, but you can't invade a planet with only a few people."

Alison shook her head. "We don't know what their overall capabilities are. My dad's symbiont, for example, can adapt to almost anything and evolve. The Battle of LA involved only a handful of Vax. From what Dad has said and some of what the government's passed on from the Nine Systems Alliance, it's not unusual for something like four to six Vax to conquer a planet if they're properly adapted."

"Bloody hell," Drysi shouted.

Ava raised a finger. "As disturbing as that possibility is, we should remember that the Tapestry have not demonstrated such high adaptation potential. Your previous encounters proved that your current strength is more than sufficient to defeat them."

"Until they get Omni," Hana muttered. She growled. "He changes all the time. That's probably the link. They want to use him to become super-freaks."

Alison nodded. "That's what I suspect. It still doesn't tell us *what* Omni is exactly, but if we have a probable idea of what motivates the Tapestry, it can help us to deal with them the next time. For now, though, everyone keep an eye and ear out. I'm not bringing in outside help other than my family, Izzie, or Lily directly. Agent Latherby knows there is a dangerous group called the Tapestry out there, and he's also keeping an eye out, even if he doesn't know what they are. If he discovered the truth, who cares?

Keeping aliens a secret is the government's policy, not mine."

"And what do we do if the Tapestry never comes back?" Hana asked.

"What we always do—security."

CHAPTER THREE

Even though the blinds were open, the dark clouds blocked most of the light and allowed only the faintest straggling rays from neighbors in the distance and the city to reach the bedroom of her island home. Alison sighed and rolled over in bed.

It wasn't the small amount of light that kept her awake. Mason slumbered beside her, his face peaceful and angelic, but that did little to soothe the doubts swirling in her head, the true source of her distress. Although everyone had reacted well to the news about her father and aliens, there was a personal discussion she still needed to have with her boyfriend.

I'm probably being paranoid, but if I don't talk to him, it'll continue to eat away at me. I need a little more focus now.

She shook his shoulder. "Hey, wake up."

He opened his eyes slowly, yawned, and squinted at her. "Is something wrong, A? Did a ward get tripped?" He tilted his head in concentration. "I don't feel anything strange."

Alison shook her head. "It's nothing like that. I've

thought we should talk for a while now and this is as good a time as ever."

The wizard rolled toward his nightstand to glance at this phone. "You wanted to talk at 2:23 AM? I'm not trying to be an asshole, but couldn't we have talked at, like, 10:00 before we went to sleep?" Weariness underlined his voice but no obvious irritation.

"Sorry. I thought I could handle it without chatting." She summoned a light orb and floated it above them. The soft glow illuminated both their faces. "I tried to let something go, but I couldn't and now, we're awake at two in the morning."

Mason chuckled and opened his eyes fully. He stretched. "Alison Brownstone couldn't let something go and is reaching out to someone rather than trying to force herself to handle it? Someone, call the Fixer. We have a shocking and unique magical development in all of history. This might be a bigger deal than the gates starting to open."

"You're sarcastic when you're sleepy." She rolled her eyes. "I'm being serious here."

He shuffled up and rested his back against the headboard. "Okay, I'm here. What's wrong, A? Talk to me. You always can. Preferably not at two in the morning, but that ship's already sailed."

"You haven't mentioned my dad since we talked this morning." She shrugged. "I'm a little surprised."

"What about your dad?" He frowned and confusion crept onto his face.

Alison pointed to the ceiling. "I told you he's an alien, and you barely blinked. I expected…more, and you took it all in stride."

"I don't understand." His frown deepened. "Did you want me to freak out? Isn't it a good thing I'm fine?"

"No, I didn't want you to freak out, but I thought it would freak you out more. At least a little." She lay down and stared at the ceiling. "You're not concerned at all? You'd be marrying into an alien family. That's weird, even for magicals."

"It doesn't really have any special implications." Mason grinned. "Your dad was already your dad when we met, and his reputation is based on what people already believe —that he's a human who uses a magical artifact. Besides, he's not your biological dad, so it's not like him being an alien will affect any kids we have or anything. We're already a strange couple in many ways, so adding a little more weirdness doesn't seem like a big deal to me."

She sighed. "Do you really think so? I keep trying to tell myself that, but it's hard to convince that little voice in the back of my head."

"Yes, I do. Or maybe we're the future of what couples will be like on Earth. I won't pretend learning that non-Oriceran aliens are real isn't surprising, but after everything we've been through together, it simply doesn't worry me that much." He smiled at her. "I think you should give up, A."

"Give up?" Alison asked. "What do you mean?"

"I think because of what happened in the past, you're always waiting for something bad to happen that you can stop. But we've all had bad things happen, especially because we're magicals in dangerous jobs, but you aren't a teenager trying to stop bad guys with your friends. You're a powerful, trained woman with highly skilled friends, and that's before you consider the fact that you can call your super-Dad to come and kick butt if you need to."

"You make it sound so normal. Like it doesn't matter."

"Because it doesn't matter." Mason shrugged. "I love you, and as long as you love me, that's all I care about. The details are exactly that…details. I don't care that your dad is an alien. I don't care about your mom's past." His smile widened. "When we first started dating, it wasn't exactly like your reputation was of some sweet, harmless woman who was never involved in any trouble and liked to mind her own business." He laughed. "If I wanted some perfectly safe woman who was never involved in trouble, I would date a perfectly safe woman and not live with and work for you. I've had enough chances to run away, and I've never taken them. I'm not leaving, no matter what. You should accept that."

"I know, but it still makes me feel better to hear you say it." Alison released a sigh of relief. "It is hard for me. You're right. In a way, I'm still trying to escape the shadow of the past. The dark wizards who screwed with me at school and my friends. What Carlyle did to me. The people hunting my dad. Even my mom having to deal with reinventing herself after all her darkness. All of it makes me question whether anything can last—if someone like me can simply be happy without complications." She turned to face him. "I'm starting to accept that it can, but what can I say? I'm a slow learner. There's also…" She shook her head.

"Don't clam up on me now, A." He frowned. "Tell me and we can work it out, no matter what it is."

"I keep meeting with Rasila," she explained. "It's strange when I think about it. We meet like girlfriends who know each other from work and not two Drow princesses who have fought one another."

"So what?" He shrugged. "That's a good thing. She's helping you, even if it is for her own reasons. I don't see the problem. She's obviously not planning some long-play ambush and has had more than one opportunity to target you again. She might not be your friend, but at least she's not an enemy."

"The more I meet with her, the more convinced I become that I won't be able to sit this Drow stuff out long-term, no matter how much I keep telling myself that I will." She shook her head. "Maybe it won't come to the boil for a few years, but I don't think I can keep pretending I can stay out of it. And that means ending up involved in a potential civil war. Rasila's first attack made it clear that you will all be involved."

"We know the risks of working for you, and we all accept them." Mason took a deep breath and nodded. "And does it matter? Can't you continue to support the status quo?"

"Supporting the status quo means supporting the Guardians. I know it doesn't sound like such a big deal, but it means I'm effectively supporting a radical change to how the Drow are governed." Alison frowned. "That's become increasingly clear to me. I'm not saying I have a strong opinion for or against them, but I have to be careful not to project a human American experience onto a non-human race from another world with a radically different history."

"That sounds reasonable," he replied. "And just to be sure, you don't want to be queen? I'm not saying you should, but you already have at least one person who is willing to support you."

Alison grimaced. "No. Absolutely not. I'm not ashamed of my Drow side, and my Drow power is useful and something I'm grateful for, but I'm also realistic about not being connected to their culture until recently. Even at the School of Necessary Magic, I spent time reading about it, not actually being around them. The other Drow might believe that because of my strong magic, I should be queen, but I don't believe that. Laena was strong, too, and she led them down a twisted path."

He frowned. "But you're not her. Her problem wasn't her power. Your dad is proof that someone can be powerful and not be a sadistic dick."

"I know. I'm merely saying being strong and being a good leader are two different things."

Mason looked aside for a moment with a slight grin. "So you have to run a security business with several teams, including an elite team of magicals with a diverse background. You have to worry about Drow politics, and you still have to stop a mysterious group who may or may not be aliens, but—at the very least—are dangerous and more than willing to kill people. Just another day in the life of Alison Brownstone. So what if you add Drow royal politics to it?"

Alison laughed. "When you say it like that, it makes me sound like such a freak. Maybe I should quit and work at my dad's restaurant."

His grin broadened. "And remember, before that, you worried about a decades-old dark wizard conspiracy, an anti-magical biological weapon and not one, but two, billionaires who conspired against you. There were also the various organized crime groups who threatened you and your friends."

She shook her head. "Are you trying to cheer me up or to depress me?"

"My point is that you've made it through all this stuff and you're stronger than ever. Whatever challenge this city throws at you, you conquer it with ease. I hope you appreciate that."

"Not without losses." She sighed as she recalled Myna's last moments. "I've lost people, and I don't want to pretend I haven't or ignore their sacrifice."

"I know, A, and we've all lost people." Mason frowned. "But all we can do is keep moving on and remember why those sacrifices were made. If you don't continue after someone's fallen in the battle, you render their sacrifice worthless."

"You sound like my dad now," she muttered.

"So, you're saying I'm offering ancient alien wisdom?"

She hit his head with her pillow. "Quiet, you."

He smiled. "Seriously, though, are you okay now? Do you get where I'm coming from?"

Alison recovered her pillow, plumped it up, and rested her head on it. "Yeah. I get that some of this is simply me looking for trouble. It's annoying. Tapestry hasn't provided an easy target for us, so my frustration boils out in other ways. Maybe we should take as many small jobs as we can —something to keep my mind off things until we can finish them off."

"It wouldn't hurt. Not everything's always a big conspiracy in need of a Dark Princess." He shrugged. "I know Jerry's team can handle most of the easy stuff, but it might be nice to simply escort a few businessmen who are worried about nothing."

"It could be." She nodded slowly. "I still think I'll check with Vincent tomorrow. It's been a couple of weeks since we last talked. Maybe he's heard of something out there that will give us a lead on the Tapestry. It wouldn't hurt. There's no way they can hide from everyone."

Mason laughed. "So your idea of relaxing is to do a ton of easy jobs but still ask your informants if they can find the evil organization hunting your friends? In other words, you don't really plan to relax at all."

She snuggled under the blanket. "Unless I hide in the World in Between, I'll never be able to clock out entirely. My dad opened a restaurant and he still ends up having to fight people. That thing in Colorado, for example, not to mention the incident in Chile."

"Okay, then." He shuffled down to lie beside her. "Maybe you should open a restaurant and bring on the sushi battle conspiracy."

"Don't tempt me."

CHAPTER FOUR

Alison bounded up the stairs at the True Portal, her ears already protected from the overwhelming cacophony of the loud music bouncing around the packed room. Given the sheer volume of flesh pressed together that night, calling it a dance club was a misnomer. It was a meat market. She didn't understand the fun of basically swaying with a sweaty mob, but she hadn't gone there for recreation. Even the bright lights and winged people who hovered above approached swarm level.

This place is so popular but it's definitely not my style.

When she reached the top of the stairs, she frowned. Vincent sat at a table, clad in a ridiculous bright purple suit, his hair so slicked and rigid that magic might be involved. His neck must have strained under the Fort Knox-level of heavy golden chains. The questionable taste in fashion and his penchant for pimpwear didn't disturb her, but the obvious and unusual presence of over a dozen suited guards did.

The men were a mixture of humans and Oricerans,

including a few Light Elves and Wood Elves. Several slid their hands toward their jackets and glared at her. No one else sat in the area.

What the hell is going on?

She paused at the top of the stairs with a frown and almost summoned a shield before she decided against it. Vincent wasn't the kind of man to make a mess at his preferred hangouts. If the guards were there as part of a plot to assassinate her, they would have already had their weapons out and made the attempt. Her informant knew her capabilities very well and unlike some people in the city, he was unlikely to ever underestimate her.

Slowly and cautiously, she took a few steps forward. "Is this a bad time?" she called. "When I sent you that message, you didn't seem to have a problem."

Vincent shook his head and gestured toward an empty chair across from him. Alison hesitated before she strolled over to the chair and glanced at the guards to rank them mentally in terms of potential difficulty. The elves would likely be the bigger threats if trouble started. A quick blinding spell would be the preferred strategy but starting a fight in a packed club risked too much collateral damage. Perhaps a better tactic would be to evade the enemy and engage them outside.

Please don't choose tonight to be an idiot, Vincent. I might not consider you a friend, but it's not like I want to have to kill you.

The informant ran a hand through his blond hair and the smile on his face looked unusually forced. "Good evening, Dark Princess. It always brightens my night when you deign to pay me a visit, and I was happy to receive your message that you wanted to meet. I always strive to be of service, especially to you."

She nodded at a nearby guard. "You always have a little muscle with you, but you don't tend to have an army. What's up with that? That has to cut into the profit margin."

"Sometimes, a man wants to feel like a king. Is that so wrong?" His eyebrow raised in query. "And sometimes, it's good to remind other people that the king has resources."

"It's your money and your ego to manage. Who am I to judge?" She shrugged. "I merely wanted to check in with you. Like I told you last time, I've been taking it easy, but that doesn't mean I don't want to head problems off before they worsen. Knowing they're out there is a necessary part of accomplishing exactly that which, in turn, makes people like you necessary. So congrats, Vincent. I'm saying you're a key part of me keeping this city safe."

He chuckled and placed a hand over his chest. "It warms my heart that you think I'm necessary."

"We all have our role in this complex web called society. Mine merely involves a little more butt-kicking than most."

Vincent smirked. "That's one way to put it, Dark Princess."

Something's wrong. Something's off, and not only the goon squad. What am I missing?

Alison looked around for a moment. None of the guards had attempted to retrieve their wands or guns. In fact, most weren't even watching her anymore and instead, focused on the stairs.

So they really are guards, not assassins.

He leaned forward. "I have a freebie for you, actually. A bonus. Since we both have our role in this web of society as you put it."

She frowned. "Since when are you a charity? When the greedy man gives away something for free, people should check their wallets."

"You're right." He nodded. "I'm not a charity. I'm a businessman, and as such, I worry about things that can affect my bottom line. Chaos is good for an information broker, but only to a point." His too-slick smile vanished. "But too much trouble isn't good for anyone, especially me. Information only flows readily in a city with a certain equilibrium, which is one of the reasons I do the job I do—to help maintain that."

Alison folded her arms. Why did she feel like she'd need a shower after meeting with Vincent?

"And someone's coming in to disrupt the equilibrium?" she asked. "Or are you only being self-important?"

"The word on the street is that Alphonse Tatum's back in town," he explained and his mouth curled in a sneer. "As of last week. We both know the kind of trouble that man can bring. I don't care that he's twisted, but I do care that he's twisted in a way that might affect me."

She nodded. Among other things, Alphonse Tatum had helped develop a dangerous potion that was functionally a weapon of mass destruction. Even though the Brownstone team had made sure it was disposed of, the fact that something like that even existed was enough to fuel a few sleepless nights.

"Do the authorities know?" she asked. "If he's that dangerous, maybe they should handle him. I'm sure the

PDA and the FBI both have a long list of questions they'd like to ask him."

"I've let a few anonymous tips reach the right ears." Vincent scoffed. "I don't care who eliminates him, but that freak will get people killed if he continues with some of his experiments. And if it happens to be you who deals with him, that's fine. But if it's some cop with a railgun, same difference to the rest of us."

"And what's Tatum doing here? Is he looking for Raven?"

"Nah, she's still staying far enough away from town." Vincent snickered. "She's almost as bad as him. Then again, you know that, don't you?"

Alison rolled her eyes. She wouldn't let him bait her about Raven being an old flame of Mason's. That whole situation was settled.

"You didn't answer the first question," she insisted.

He shrugged. "I can't be sure, but I have an idea." He licked his lips.

She suddenly realized what was off. The man didn't have his signature magical martini.

Those guards aren't about showing off. He's nervous and off his game and habits. But why?

"An idea? A few details would be nice." She wasn't eager to go after someone as dangerous as Alphonse Tatum while the threat of the Tapestry still hung in the air. At the same time, she also didn't need any new magical chemical weapons threatening her city, and she could always direct the PDA at him.

Vincent's mouth twitched, and his nose wrinkled with disgust. He leaned forward and lowered his voice. It was unnecessary given the sound-absorbing bubble he always kept around his table—which made her suspect it was sheer reflex and another example of him being nervous. Everything he did, wore, and said had a distinct and planned purpose. He was a performer, but something had spooked the performance almost out of him.

"Your dad did many people a favor in Vegas when he stopped Ultimate there," he continued. "I don't mind a man getting high, but a man warping himself like that? It's… unnatural. The kinds of men involved in using a drug like that are those who don't respect stability. They are bad for business for anyone other than the Ultimate dealers." He frowned. "That's the thing. You stirred the pot in the beginning, but everything was settling down around you. Now, people are coming and stirring the pot again."

"Ultimate?" Alison frowned. "What does Ultimate have to do with Tatum?"

"This is something I've kept close while I looked into it." Vincent spread his hands in front of him. "Because I wanted to be sure, and this is a situation where I need to be careful who I tell. I don't want to end up with unnecessary enemies."

"I'm still not following you, Vincent."

"Last week, there was a raid on an Eastern Union storehouse," he explained. "The guy killed four Union men before they finally killed him, and they had deflectors and antimagic bullets. He was a minor wizard tough who worked mostly out of Portland—a hired gun who wasn't that powerful. I bet one of the freshmen at your school could have outspelled him, but the thing is, when he attacked that warehouse, he was way more powerful than anyone's ever seen him before, and he'd changed. Some of the survivors said his eyes were different and his body was twisted and weird."

Alison grimaced. "He was using Ultimate."

Vincent nodded. "And don't you find it convenient that Tatum comes back to town at about the same time we suddenly have our first case of Ultimate in the entire Pacific Northwest?"

"Yeah, that does seem questionable." She glanced over her shoulder, suddenly more suspicious. "But I don't understand why you'll tell the cops and PDA—or whoever you told—about Tatum, but you're afraid to go to them with this information."

He gestured toward the dance floor. "Tatum didn't come to town to fling some wizard cannon fodder at the Eastern Union, and he'll either get killed, arrested, or eventually leave. But if he's the one dealing Ultimate, then he *ultimately* needs customers, right? People who are here and might not take too kindly if someone inadvertently sent the cops or feds at them, including entire organizations, but you..." He shrugged. "Everyone understands the Dark Princess has to control her kingdom. So, that's the thing—keeping this info underground is part of the price for this information."

"I thought you said this was free." She frowned. "Now you're attaching strings?"

"It is free. I'm not asking you to pay, but I am asking you to keep the cops and PDA out of this for now. In exchange, I'll make sure you know about anything that's going on with Ultimate. But if you involve the cops, you obviously trust their information and you don't need mine."

She scowled in concentration as she considered the offer. It wasn't as if she would prevent the authorities from investigating. She merely wouldn't give them an active helping hand. They had their own resources and informants. Their investigations wouldn't dry up without the assistance of the Dark Princess. In the end, she was usually someone they brought to serve as the hammer at the end of an investigation rather than a magnifying glass at the beginning.

She gestured toward a few of the guards. "Is that what all of this is about? You're worried that an Ultimate mutant might attack you?"

Vincent responded with a crooked smile. "No, this is merely…an unrelated matter. Don't worry, Dark Princess. It doesn't involve you. Not everything in Seattle does, even if it seems that way at times."

Alison grinned. "Before, you said it was about showing off. You gave something up and got nothing out of it. Sloppy, Vincent. You're off your game tonight."

He shook a finger at her. "Good catch. You keep my info with you and yours, and I'll let you know about any possible Ultimate leads. If you want to turn them over to the cops after you kick a little ass, that's fine, as long as you keep my name out of it."

"Fair enough." She stood. "Thanks, Vincent."

"As always." He mocked-bowed. "All hail the Dark Princess."

Alison rolled her eyes. "You're lucky you're so useful."

"Those words will go on my tombstone," he called in reply.

She turned and strolled past the guards to the stairs. The arrival of Ultimate in Seattle was unsettling but not surprising. It had been only a matter of time, but the fact that the police were behind the information curve was telling. That really did suggest powerful factions were doing what they could to advance their agendas with the drug before the authorities could stop them.

I guess I have something to take my mind off the Tapestry, but it sounds even more annoying.

The wizard licked his lips and rubbed his hands together. He forced himself to stay on the couch in the small room despite how much he wanted to pace. Power. It'd be his soon as long as he received his delivery.

The click of heels on concrete echoed down the hallway outside. He took a deep breath and glanced at two vials of blood on the small brown table in front of him. It was an odd price and it'd taken some doing to obtain blood from both a Gray Elf and a gnome, but it would be worth it.

The footsteps drew closer and a woman appeared in the doorway. She was tall with a beautiful heart-shaped face. Her long silver hair cascaded down her back and complimented her piercing silver eyes. Her belted black trench coat covered her body and black leather gloves concealed her hands, but given the chilly late winter temperature, that wasn't surprising. The wizard was disappointed for the most basic and carnal of reasons. A woman with that beautiful a face probably had a body to match.

"Are you Mirela?" he asked.

The woman nodded and closed the door behind her. She slid a hand into her pocket, removed something folded in a small piece of paper, and held it out in her palm.

"You know the terms of the exchange?" Mirela asked, a faint accent underlying her words. The man neither knew nor cared what kind it was.

"I've heard, yeah." He nodded. "If we don't say anything about where this came from, we can get another dose. Otherwise, we're iced." He reached over to grab the paper, unfolded it, and frowned. While he'd never actually seen Ultimate before, he'd heard it described. It usually came as a small pill. Instead, the paper contained a small spiky black crystal.

"Is there a problem?" she asked.

"What is this?" the wizard asked. "I wanted Ultimate. How can I even swallow this? It'll shred my throat."

"This is Ultimate," she replied. "It's merely in its purer form. My employer feels this will be more satisfying to our customer base."

He shook his head. "No, no, no. Ultimate's already risky. I won't be your guinea pig." He held the crystal out. "The deal's off."

Her gaze dropped to the vials. "I've come for that blood. My employer needs it."

"The deal's off, I said." The wizard shrugged. "Look, maybe we can work a deal in a few weeks. I want to wait and see what happens with this new version of Ultimate before I risk myself. I understand there are always side-effects, but this might be more dangerous."

Mirela frowned, clearly displeased. "I don't understand. We had a deal. I risked myself coming here and now, you say you don't want the product?"

"Yeah." He shook his hand at her. "You keep it."

She snatched the crystal from his hand and opened her mouth, dropped it down her throat, and swallowed. Her head jerked and she twitched a few times before her veins darkened and she uttered a slight gasp. The veins returned to normal a few seconds later. "You're a fool."

He grimaced. "Haven't you ever heard you shouldn't use your own product?"

"It's hard." She took a step toward him and raised her right hand. "The more you take, the more your mind whispers strange things. Are the fingers the hand, or is the hand the fingers?"

"What? Huh? What are you talking about?" The man took a step back. Ultimate was rapidly losing its appeal.

"Don't worry." Mirela drew a few deep breaths. Her cheeks grew flushed. "My employer will solve that problem. All advancements have initial failures and side-effects. Power can never be easily seized by the weak."

"Okay, I'm done." He turned toward the table and retrieved the vials. "This deal's definitely off. I'm not interested."

She threw a gloved hand in front of him. "Because you're weak and short-sighted."

"Lady, I was stupid to even look into Ultimate. I don't want to end up frying my brain. I only wanted a little more juice."

"You don't have to worry about frying your brain," she whispered. "It'll no longer be a problem."

The wizard scoffed. "You're not exactly a stunning example of that."

Mirela yanked her right glove off. Her entire hand was covered with tiny silver crystals.

"What the hell?" He shook his head. "Some prices aren't worth paying."

"Perhaps," she replied.

He pushed past her. "I'm sorry I ever even asked."

"You should be."

The man took two more steps before he screamed in agony as fiery pain seared through his chest. He looked down. Mirela had stabbed completely through his chest with her hand.

"It's unfortunate your essence isn't more special," she murmured. "But at least now, you won't have to worry about your brain." She yanked her hand back. "Don't you understand? I'm free of even a wand and more powerful than most Oricerans."

The wizard coughed blood and collapsed. He tried to reach for his wand, but she pinned his hand with the heel of her knee-high dark boot.

"Becoming something greater always means casting off weakness," she whispered and smiled at him as his life slowly drained out.

CHAPTER FIVE

Maybe I'm more of a danger junkie than I knew, Alison thought. *I should never have agreed to do this. But I'm more annoyed than bored.*

She sighed and took another sip of her coffee as she glanced around the Forbidden Bean coffee shop. Various people chatted over their bagels, cookies, and coffee. Her gaze surveyed the room and lingered on a young couple. They were around her age, albeit far more elegantly dressed, and sat in a booth chatting happily. The man gesticulated wildly. She sat so the woman's back was to her and had made a point of entering the shop only after the couple was seated. Avoiding her field of view had been easy enough, even without magic.

This was a terrible idea.

Hana sat opposite Mason at another table across the room. Both pretended to look at their phones while they drank coffee. Every other customer was a Brownstone Security employee—most from Jerry's team and a few of the office staff—all dressed in normal clothes. Other than the couple and the barista, her people controlled the entire building.

"I'm starting to really regret taking this job," she whispered. She pulled her phone out and brought it to her ear so she looked less like she was talking to herself, even though she only had to fool two people in the entire room.

"Why?" Tahir replied through her hidden ear receiver. "It's remarkably well-paying for so little effort, and isn't it consistent with your goal of relaxing for a few weeks while we look into the other matters? I admit it isn't as stimulating as our normal work, but at least it won't involve anyone dying."

"If this plan fails, the guy will die from embarrassment," Hana muttered.

Alison sighed. "But this isn't even security work. Not really. I shouldn't put on a show for some random guy. I won't say it's beneath us, but...I honestly don't know."

"Consider it public relations," the fox whispered over the comms. "Besides, it'll make him happy. You heard the message Ava received. He's a huge fan. You're doing him the favor of the lifetime."

I thought I was done with this kind of thing when I moved out of the condo. I'm lucky Ryan doesn't still follow me around and now, I have super-fans calling the company?

"I'm not a freaking celebrity," she muttered. "I don't need to be part of cutesy 'and then I met Alison Brownstone' stories."

"In a purely factual sense, that's not true," the infomancer replied.

"Huh? What are you talking about?"

"You are a celebrity." He scoffed quietly. "You're probably one of the higher-profile celebrities in the area, even if you're not an entertainer. You're famous and people follow your activities closely. Yes, many celebrities attempt to garner that status for themselves, but many others have it thrust upon them."

It's easy for him to be relaxed. He gets to sit back in his office and do nothing but drone the area. I'm the one who has to embarrass herself.

"Do we really need this kind of PR?" she countered. "Helping a guy propose? I…ugh."

When the request came in, she wanted to reject it out of hand, but the lingering memory of her father's painful and lengthy quest to craft the perfect epic proposal stayed her hand. She'd hesitated long enough for arguments on behalf of aiding a man to convince her to help his attempt, complete with the Dark Princess making an appearance.

I don't know if Dad would approve or disapprove. He gives autographs, so it's not like he's completely disgusted with the idea of people coming to him because he's famous. And I'm not doing this because of ego.

"Why are you so concerned?" Mason asked. "It's only a fun little game. We didn't have to travel far."

She glanced at him and he smirked at her.

So it's giving you ideas, huh? Maybe I should pull a Mom and force you into something elaborate, too.

"Because this is one step away from doing things like commercial endorsement," Alison complained. "It's good to have a nice reputation, but I also need to have a certain reputation with the underworld." She allowed herself a moment to take a deep breath after her voice grew too loud. "And I don't want them thinking I've gone soft," she murmured.

He chuckled. "Your dad was doing barbecue stuff well before he retired, and no one ever said that made him look weak. It's not like the underworld will release a horde of assassins because you helped someone out."

"This isn't the same thing." She shook her head.

"Even if they did," Hana interjected, "we'd kick their butts and then they'd talk about how 'Don't mess with Alison after she helped someone propose.' This is fun, like the commercials. You used to like acting. Think of it as adding acting into security." She gasped. "Security theater. I invented something new."

"I don't think that means what you think." Tahir chuckled.

"Oh, be quiet, babe."

Alison groaned. "I'm surprised that Ava, of all people, suggested we do this. She's the one I depend on to be straightforward and rational."

"See? That proves it." Hana snickered. "If Super Mary Poppins says it's a good idea, it has to be. Don't be such a chicken."

"I'm not a chicken."

"You have wings," the fox countered.

"And horses have tails. Does that make you nine horses?"

The woman giggled loudly enough to draw the attention of the client's girlfriend, who eyed her with a curious look.

Alison glanced at the time on her phone. There were only a few minutes before it was time for the client to pop the question. Her part was simple and her employees would be loud with their cheers. She would pose for pictures with the couple, complete with shadow wings. A nice, simply PR op in theory, but she couldn't get the rest of her brain to agree. Maybe it was because Drysi had already opted out after arguing that a former dark wizard assassin might not be something the company wanted to emphasize in PR jobs.

The door chime sounded, and a man in a loose flannel shirt and ballcap stepped inside. A small amount of magic radiated from him and a wand was tucked into his back pocket.

Alison rolled her eyes. It wasn't all that long ago that wizards were special men and their wands were specials tool. Now, they might still be rarer than the average person, but random punks with wands filled every city and made a mockery of magic. She frowned and remembered the plan, but no one had mentioned the unexpected arrival.

Who is he?

"There's a problem," Tahir reported, his tone serious.

"What?" she asked.

"The gentleman who just entered," the infomancer explained. "He literally appeared out of thin air right before he stepped inside."

"He likes to be flashy, huh?" she muttered.

The man pulled his wand out and shouted an incantation. A small fireball careened upward and blew a smoking hole into a ceiling tile. All the Brownstone Security employees fell silent and looked at him. Hana and Mason locked their attention on the man but didn't make a move.

Oh no, no, no.

"Please tell me this is part of the show," Alison whispered.

"Not to the best of my knowledge," Tahir replied. "But Jerry did say there might be a few surprises. We should have wired him into the comms. Hindsight, alas, only helps you in future battles."

"This is what happens when you don't coordinate," she muttered. "I knew we should have had a formal script."

"Okay, you latte-drinking assholes, listen up," the wizard bellowed. "Give me all your jewelry." With his free hand, he yanked out a small black device with a black and silver slot. "And I'll take a little scan of your cards, too. This is a little something we real Seattleites like to call a robbery."

The couple looked at the man. While the woman's eyes widened in concern, the man grinned.

So he was expecting it?

Alison tried not to burst into laughter.

Is this guy for real? He's overacting. Like to call a robbery? Please. I suppose I should give the client a show, then.

She stood and summoned a shield. The wizard jerked his head toward her and glared.

"What are you doing, bitch?" he snarled. "You'd better watch yourself."

If the man was an actor, he had gone a little over the top, but the fireball hadn't been an illusion, either. She frowned.

Oh, crap.

Jerry was near the front and she glanced quickly at him. He frowned and shook his head.

You're kidding me. He actually is a robber?

"You have an easy choice here," she said calmly. "You can choose to walk away." She shook her head lightly at Hana and Mason, both poised to spring out of their seats. Any sudden movements might end with trouble, and no one else had defense artifacts or anti-magic deflectors. She was the only one with a shield in the whole room.

"I'm not walking away," the wizard yelled. "I came here to get paid!"

The girlfriend of their client trembled and sagged in her chair, her eyes wide in terror.

Alison sighed. "Don't you recognize me, you idiot?"

"Idiot? I'm the one with his wand out, bitch." The man studied her arrogantly. "Who the hell are you supposed to be?"

I told everyone I'm not a celebrity. Half the time, people don't recognize me when I need them to. He wouldn't have asked who I was if I was Jericho Cartwright.

"I'm Alison Brownstone." She frowned. "And I was in the middle of something that you interrupted. So I'd like you to turn around and leave, or I can make you do so. It's your choice."

The robber stepped back, his jaw tight. He pointed his wand at her. "You're lying. There's no way I would walk into someplace and have Alison Brownstone be there."

"Really?" She rolled her eyes. "This is the Forbidden Bean. It's right around the corner from a building with my name on it. Don't you pay attention to anything?" She threw her hands up in frustration. "What? Did you pick a place to rob at random?"

He shrugged. "It wasn't totally at random. Well…the neighborhood wasn't random."

She rubbed a hand down her face. "I can't believe this. Get out. Now." She gestured around. "Almost everyone in this room works for me. You cannot rob this place successfully. You'll be lucky if you don't get hurt."

"Y-you can't be her." The wizard shook his head. "It's a bluff."

"Hana, fox out," Alison ordered.

The other woman stood. Her eyes turned vulpine and her nine glowing tails appeared in an instant. She uttered a low growl as her claws extended and.

His eyes widened and he swallowed.

Alison pointed her thumb at Hana. "Do you know many other people who have a nine-tailed fox working for them in Seattle? Hell, do you know *anyone* else in this country who has a nine-tailed fox working for them?"

"I—" The wizard jerked his wand from one woman to the other and back again. "Back off." He took a few steps toward the entrance, which moved him closer to where Jerry sat with three other men.

Jerry looked over at her with a questioning look on his face. She nodded. When men were well-trained, they didn't need explicit orders.

"What are you nodding at?" the wizard barked.

"Time's up," she declared. "Not your luckiest day. Sorry."

Her team leapt from the table and tackled him as a group. One of the security operators snatched the man's wand from his hand and tossed it onto the floor. It rolled a yard way. Within seconds, the would-be robber lay flat on his stomach and howled in pain when his arm was bent back by a scowling Jerry.

Alison marched over and knelt in front of him. "You didn't even have a shield up? They probably still would have taken your wand, but...pathetic." She shook her head and placed her hand on his forehead. After a quick incantation, her hand glowed. The wizard's eyes closed, and he slumped, unconscious.

The client bolted to his feet and clapped. "That's what I'm talking about. Brownstone Security kicking butt! Boo yah!"

She turned toward him, unsure whether he realized an actual attempted robbery had occurred or if he still thought it was all part of a show.

He retrieved a ring box from his back pocket and fell to one knee in front of his girlfriend. "This near-death experience has made it clear to me that I can't last one more minute without you at my side. Will you do me the honor of being my wife?"

Near-death experience? That's a bit much.

The woman blinked and looked from Alison to her boyfriend before she plucked the ring from the box. "Of course I will!"

Everyone cheered and clapped. Several whistled.

Alison shook her head and chuckled quietly. "No more PR jobs."

CHAPTER SIX

The setting sun dipped below the trees in the distance. Frosty temperatures still lingered in the area, but a few recent spikes during the day heralded the coming spring. Alison sat on the edge of the pier in front of her home, enjoying the cool caress of the February wind on her cheeks. A good jacket was all she needed for comfort. She enjoyed the cold sometimes. It could focus her mind. With everything going on lately, a little focus wasn't a bad thing.

She took a deep breath and pressed the call button on her phone. All the madness swirling around Seattle and the company forced her into almost selfish myopia, but she had other responsibilities, including to the parents who had saved her when she needed it most. All the strange organizations and drugs in the world would never change that, and she would never let herself forget.

"Hey, Alison," Shay answered. "What's up?"

"I wanted to check on you," she explained with a smile. "The last time we talked a couple of weeks ago, I kind of got the feeling you were angry about something. Since I was the one doing most of the talking, I thought maybe I was the problem. I didn't want to press you about it and decided I'd give you a couple of weeks to cool off, but now I think that was a mistake."

"Angry?" Her mother sighed. "Where did you get that idea? Wait. Oh, I get it. I'm sorry, Alison."

"No, I'm sorry if I made you mad, Mom," she replied. "I know your hormones are probably going crazy with the baby and all, and I shouldn't call you and dump my personal problems on you. That's not fair."

The other woman laughed. "What a messed-up family we have if stuff like, 'Hey, Mom, these weird crazy guys who eat magic crystals are hunting me' is something you consider a 'personal problem.' The whole point of family is to have each other's back, especially in our case because we chose to be family. We both know how important that is."

"I'm not saying the Tapestry aren't important, but they're also not your problem. Since I decided to go off on my own, the last thing I want to do is drag everyone into my business. If that's what happens, I could have simply kept working for Brownstone Agency." She sighed. "I'm the one who chose to become a security contractor, and I'm the one who chooses to stick my nose into everyone's business up here. I shouldn't complain that a dangerous line of work leads to dangerous situations with strange magicals, especially to you, of all people. You decided your personal tolerance for danger and changed jobs—twice, at that—even if you still stick your feet in the tomb raiding pool now and again."

"You still don't understand, Alison. I'm not mad at you

at all." Shay's voice grew softer. "I don't think I've been truly mad at you in a long, long time. Now, your dad? He pisses me off all the time with his OCD-ness and general obtuse nature, but even that doesn't really get me mad. I married him, after all, and I had many chances to run away and fake my death again."

Alison laughed. "That's an interesting way to put it."

"He's been great about the baby since his road trip," Shay continued. "Now, you actually did sense something last time I called. I shouldn't be surprised, even though I always am." She chuckled. "Even without your soul sight, you've always been good at that kind of thing. I remember how we used to always have trouble with that when we called you at school, especially when we didn't want to tell you the truth about some stupid thing your dad was caught up in. For a while, both he and I were convinced you had some sort of spell that let you sense our emotions at a distance. I don't know if it's from growing up with soul sight or simply because you care so much, but you've always been overly sensitive and caring when it comes to those close to you. That can be annoying when we're trying to protect you from something."

She frowned. "Mom, I don't think it's possible to be too sensitive and caring toward your loved ones, and I still don't understand. From what you've said, it sounds like there was something wrong last time you called. I don't need to be protected. I'm older now, and I have control of my powers. I want to be the one to protect you."

"There was something wrong," the woman admitted, "but not with you, with me. That's what I'm getting at.

There's no deep conspiracy or deadly threat, merely an overly emotional mother."

"There's not something wrong with the baby, is there?" Alison gasped and her heart rate kicked up. There were some things that even having the power of a Drow princess wouldn't help her with, and the wish was now long gone.

Please, please, please.

"Nope," Shay responded cheerfully. "Nothing remotely wrong. We have some of the best doctors in the country, if not the planet, helping us with this, and more than a few witches and wizards who have offered their help, including Zoe." She scoffed. "I assume the doctor is giving tissue samples to government agencies for analysis, but everyone wants this baby to be born healthy and happy and are doing their best to ensure that happens."

She exhaled a sigh of relief. "Oh, thank God. You had me worried."

"Yeah, it's nothing like that. It's just…" She sighed. "Look, Alison, you know me. I might be a professor now but being a woman of action is my nature and why I fell into my first line of work. It's also why I still can't give up the raids entirely, even though Lily is a better tomb raider than I ever was. The thing is, so much is going on with you and that makes me frustrated."

"Frustrated?" Alison frowned. "About what exactly?"

"About not being able to help you. Your dad went with you to Canada and beat those dark wizards' asses so black and blue they'll be afraid of you for centuries. Now, this crap with these Tapestry freaks is happening, and if something gets really hot, he'll be the one to help you, not me. Sure, I gave you the artifact and the car, but that's not the same thing as fighting beside you." She exhaled an even longer sigh than before. "Maybe I'm merely emotional because of the pregnancy, but I thought about the times we really bonded in the beginning—like that time I went to the school to check on you because James had gotten himself into trouble. Not that it doesn't describe every week of his life from back then."

Alison chuckled. "It is crazy now to think about how much trouble he got in, even as a bounty hunter. I remember all those times, though. I liked you from the beginning, even if you tried not to warm to me."

"I didn't want to care, you know," her mother murmured, her tone distant. "Not about you. Not about him, either, but the more time I spent around you both, the more I couldn't help it. I was a woman who prided herself on not giving a damn about anyone, and you two wormed your way into my heart. You got past all my defenses and before I knew it, I was no longer thinking about saving money and running off to some island to disappear. I was thinking about what the future would be like with both of you. It scared me, but I was never one to back down because of a little fear."

She chuckled. "You make it sound so bad."

"Not bad, merely surprising. You know what my life was like before."

"Yeah, but that was before."

"True enough."

"You don't have to worry about me up here," she assured her. "I'm not saying Dad wasn't a big help in

Canada, but I can take care of myself and I have a great team. I hate the idea that I make you worry with my job."

Shay muttered something under her breath. "You don't make me worry. I know you can handle yourself. I simply miss picking up the old sword and chopping some deserving heads off. And now that I'm having the new kid, both James and I will need to be more careful about whatever shit we are involved in. I don't even know if it's smart for him to wander off and have adventures, even with Whispy. There's always a chance that something could happen. You never know."

Alison leaned back and rested on her elbows. She stared at a few stars already twinkling in the darkening sky, the calm waters in front of her soothing. "I don't think Dad will die until barbecue is entirely destroyed. After all, virtually everyone has tried every different way, and they've always lost."

"Maybe, but the point is you're all grown up," Shay replied. "It's like you said. You have a good team. You have a successful business, and you even have a good man who seems to actually have decent emotional sense, unlike your dad. If the worst happened tomorrow and your dad and I were in trouble, whether blown up or portaled to some strange corner of Oriceran, we could die or end up there knowing you would be okay. We love you, and we know you love us, but we also know you don't really need us anymore—not like you did when you were that scared fifteen-year-old girl reeling from your entire world changing."

She grimaced. "Mom, don't talk like that. Both of you will be around for a long time—a very long time."

"I'm not saying either of us plan to do anything danger-ous, let alone plan to die," she replied. "I'm only saying it'll be a while before we're in that same position of freedom again. I'll bring this new kid into the world, and I won't saddle you with them because I was jonesing for danger. I know money won't be a problem, but you need to be free to chart your own future. You need to be free to seize your own victories and make your own mistakes. It's a sobering and beautiful thing having a child. It makes the future real and crystalizes it, and I say this as a woman who has stared death in the face any number of times. So don't you worry about me. I'll be frustrated for a while until your new sibling is old enough to go on a little adventure with your father and me. I love you, Alison, and I want to be able to help you. That's all this is."

"I love you, too, Mom, and you've already helped me more than you can possibly imagine."

CHAPTER SEVEN

A lison squatted in front of the brown iguana puttering around the office floor. Although Hana had added a litter box, several toys, and even a hamster maze, it remained a small office and not a pet palace. The other employees weren't comfortable with bringing their precious pets to stick them in a back office all day. She wasn't sure if she was relieved or annoyed by that, but for now, her focus remained on the mysterious creature in front of her.

"What are you, Omni?" she muttered. "Are you the secret king of Tapestry? The ultimate criminal? Something to make them stronger?"

Hana leaned against the door, her arms folded and a pensive look on her face. "If it turns out he's an alien, you won't give him to the government to dissect, will you? Even if he can turn all scary and 'Send in the Space Marines,' he's still my baby."

She shook her head. "I don't have a reason to think he's a threat to anyone but the Tapestry at the moment, so I have no reason to send him to the government. Those are the same people who are still messing with my dad after he saved the damned planet from an alien invasion. Senator Johnston and a couple of people like him are okay, but I trust the rest of them about as much as I trust your average technomagic billionaire."

The other woman snickered. "That's good to hear." She sighed wistfully. "I'm sorry he's causing trouble."

"He's not causing the trouble. The assholes after him are causing the trouble because they won't take no for an answer." She frowned. "I'm tired of people thinking they can push my friends and family around, and you know what? You are all part of my family now. You even know my dad's secret."

Hana grinned. "It's really cool, you know. I always thought he was impressive but knowing all the stuff about his true origins makes him even more special. He could easily have been the bad guy we had to eliminate."

Alison uttered a dark chuckle. "If that was the case, he would have kicked our asses, but I know what you mean." She pointed to her eyes. "I could still see souls back then. I knew he was a good person from the moment I saw him, even if he didn't believe it himself. He saved me, too, from my bio dad—the man who was supposed to love me and who turned his own wife over to gangsters." She frowned. "That just goes to show you. Family isn't about blood. It's about love and respect, and that's why I think of all of you as family."

The fox turned, her cheeks scarlet. "Oh. Keep it up and you'll make me cry in front of Omni."

"I've seen you cry at sad scenes in comedies." She grinned.

"I'm a very sensitive soul." Her friend winked. "It's why I made such a good con artist even without the charm. I could understand and sympathize with people."

Alison nodded. She'd not thought much about her friends' pasts lately. Drysi's continual self-flagellation concerning her history serving the Seventh Order made it harder to forget, but Hana remained a fixture in her mind. She was the faithful fox who had been with her from the beginning, just as Mason wasn't a former bodyguard but her boyfriend, now and forever. Even Tahir, who had been an arrogant ass when they'd first met, was now a valued friend and advisor.

Have they all changed? Or have I changed? Maybe we all have. We've grown together.

Omni uttered something approaching a raspy chirp and headed toward the hamster maze. He was slender enough in iguana form that he could still enjoy it.

"Sometimes, I wonder what would happen if we didn't watch him for a long time," Hana murmured and stared at the pet. "I mean for, like, months. Would he revert to a different form? Is Angry Omni his true form?"

"I think true form's a weird concept to apply to something that constantly changes shape." Alison shrugged.

"You mean like a nine-tailed fox." Her friend grinned.

"Maybe." She nodded at Omni. "But it's different. You're an intelligent being. I wonder if he's actually intelligent."

"What are you talking about? He's very smart. He can do tricks." Hana pushed away from the door. "He's the smartest pet on the planet, probably—even if he isn't from this planet—and it doesn't seem to matter what form he's in. He's as smart whatever he is."

"I mean intelligent as in can think like us." Alison gestured toward the iguana scuttling through the plastic hamster maze. "Or if he's merely an animal. It's not like he's writing out explanations for us. And he's running through a hamster maze."

The other woman scoffed. "That makes more sense than running on a treadmill."

She laughed. "You got me there, but I still wonder."

"Does it really matter?" Hana asked with a shrug. "Maybe he's intelligent but he took a vow of silence or something. For now, we only have to make sure the Tapestry doesn't get him."

"That's what's bugging me. What if he's using us?" She frowned. "What if he pretends not to be intelligent only to hide with us? It might have been a ploy from the beginning. The average person will react positively to a puppy."

"I wondered about that, but I don't think so."

"Why is that?" she asked.

The fox extended claws on one hand. "Because Angry Omni kicks plenty of ass. I don't think that's the problem, and the Tapestry are straight-up assholes." She punctuated the sentiment with a low growl. "And I'm not saying that because they tried to kill me, but that did move them to nearly the top of the list."

Alison stood. "I'm not saying they aren't bad. I'm merely trying to wrap my mind around all this. I don't know who and what they are, and that worries me. They could be aliens. They could be Oricerans. They could be weird wizards who really like themed organizational names, but whoever they are, they're dangerous."

"Why does it worry you so much?" Hana retracted her claws. "We've beaten them in a fight."

"We defeated many dark wizards in fights, too, before we faced the Seventh Order in their headquarters." Her stomach knotted and bile rose in the back of her throat. "And I thought I had a good handle on them, but Myna still died."

Her friend sighed. "Oh, Alison, that's not your fault."

"Isn't it? She died in battle against my enemies. I just... want to be more careful going forward. If there's one thing my time in Seattle has taught me, it's that the assholes don't always show their best cards at first." She clenched a hand into a fist. "And I don't want to force anyone into having to make that kind of decision again. I'm not saying she made the wrong call. Because of her sacrifice, hundreds if not thousands of innocent people were saved. But if I do my job as a leader, my allies will be able to concentrate on winning and we force the other side to have to make choices about who will sacrifice themselves."

"But the Tapestry is lying low. Nobody has to make any choices right now."

Alison pointed at Omni. "Even if they wait a few months in the hope that they can catch us off guard, they'll come back. From what they said and the way they acted, that much is clear. I know we can't always be on high alert, but we have to keep that in the back of our mind."

"All over an animal, huh?" Hana tilted her head, a soft smile on her face. "That makes me wonder."

"About?"

"It's like you said earlier. Shapeshifting. I sometimes wonder what it would be like to be a nine-tailed fox who lived in the country. Here in this big city, I spend almost all my time in human form, but maybe I'd be more in touch with my fox nature if I lived out there. It's hard to say if I'm a fox who becomes a human and has forgotten she's a fox or human who becomes a fox. You know, in the spiritual sense. That's why it's strange for me to think about whether Omni's an animal or intelligent or whatever you want to think about."

"I understand a little about being from two worlds," she replied. "It can be rough. That's for sure, even if you have other people around to support you. And—" Her phone rang. "One second." She didn't recognize the number but given her profession, she wasn't in a habit of ignoring any calls. "Hello?"

"Hello, Dark Princess," replied Vincent in a smooth voice. "I'm glad you answered so easily. I hope I caught you at an opportune time."

"It's not like you to call me directly," she stated. "You're really erratic lately, Vincent. Don't think I haven't noticed."

"Again, I applaud your attention to detail, but as I said the other day, it's not your concern."

Alison scoffed. "You're the one who called me. You need to work on your phone etiquette."

"Yes, indeed I do. Concerning that, timeliness is an issue for this particular matter." He clucked his tongue. "And don't worry, I've taken precautions. No one will be able to monitor or record this call, which will facilitate you handling an Ultimate incident."

"If it's an emergency, AET might be a better bet," she suggested.

Vincent hissed. "No cops. Not yet. I don't want to get the police involved until this is closer to the end. I've already articulated my reasons why, and I know you understand them."

"I'm just saying—"

"In a very short while," he continued and interrupted her, "there will be a raid on the headquarters of a Tacoma-area gang, the Red Bears."

Confusion swallowed her irritation over the information broker's attitude as she parsed his words.

"Did you say the Red Bears?" Alison frowned.

"Yes, the Red Bears. Do you know them?"

"Yes." She let doubt lace her voice. "I've heard of them anyway, but I've never dealt with them directly. They're nothing. They have no magic and control very little territory. I know they help provide street dealers with some Eastern Union product, and that's the sole reason they continue to exist, but they are a non-factor in the underworld. What do they have to do with Ultimate? As far as I know, Ultimate only works on magicals."

"To the best of my knowledge, that's true," Vincent admitted. "And their non-magical nature is what's made them an expendable target. I think they're intended as a demonstration. Word has leaked that a newer version of Ultimate might be on the streets. They say it's purer and more powerful, and the slaughter of the Red Bears is supposed to be proof of the quality, but I don't know. My information in this matter is spotty."

Alison scowled, still not entirely convinced as to the

plausibility of the information. "They don't think killing an entire gang will draw the police's attention?"

"I think they have measures to slow investigations, and it's not as if the police always care if criminals are eliminated. In some cases, it simply ends up being less work for them."

"I don't care. I'm calling the police. The Red Bears might be gang members, but they don't deserve to be target practice for some drug-addled wizard."

"If the police show up *before* the raid, it will point directly at me," the man explained, his voice tight. "My life will be in danger, and I will be forced to go underground. I almost am already for other reasons. If you don't want information for a while, that's your choice. Otherwise, I suggest you stop the raid yourself. Besides, I think you need to know what you're up against. Your father might have fought men on Ultimate, but not anyone using this new version."

Her jaw tightened. She didn't mind handling problems herself, but she felt like she would be pulled into something that risked spiraling out of control. Still, she needed Vincent. If the Tapestry infiltrated Seattle again, he might hear of it.

I need to deepen my informant base, but it is what it is.

"Fine," she muttered. "Give me the address. If it's Tacoma, I should be able to fly there in time."

Vincent rattled off the number. "Make good choices, because all choices have consequences." He ended the call.

"Damn it," Alison yelled.

Omni glanced at her before he resumed his scuttling.

"What's wrong?" Hana looked concerned.

"Drysi and Mason aren't here, and I'm on a time limit." She stormed toward the door. "I'll have to fly there directly."

"I heard you mention the Red Bears and Ultimate. What's going on? I'm here. I can help."

"Just someone stirring up trouble." She sighed. "I can fly there faster than we can drive. You stay here. There's still the chance that something else will pop up."

Damn it. If only I could portal. Myna said I needed to work on my shadow compression, but she's gone. That's another reason to reconsider asking Rasila for more help.

The fox frowned. "I don't like the idea of you going somewhere by yourself and fighting some magical junkie."

"Tahir can send tactical drones to back me up," she responded as she threw the door open. "But I have to move now."

CHAPTER EIGHT

The people were a blur of muted dark colors beneath her as Alison streaked through the sky. She poured more magical energy into her wings to increase speed toward the junkyard the Red Bears used as their base. Although she was unsure about not contacting the police, she couldn't risk alienating Vincent. The informant was already skittish enough, and she still needed him.

Is he that worried about Ultimate? He keeps acting like there's something else going on. Maybe he's spooked about Tatum, but it sounded like he was more than willing to give the man up if he could. I'm missing something.

She was now only a few minutes from the destination. The roads below were jam-packed with vehicles. If she had attempted to drive with Hana, there was no way they would have made it there in time.

Faster. I need to go faster. This might be my chance to get a direct line on the source of Ultimate and cut it off like Dad did in Las Vegas.

In theory, she had no top speed as long as she could continue to draw on magic, but even she had her limits. She gritted her teeth as she shoved even more of her power into her wings. After a sharp turn, she located the junkyard in the distance where heaped piles of metal formed their own miniature model of the Cascades. She drew a deep breath and layered shields over herself before she released some of the magic that sustained her forward momentum. The natural air resistance slowed her before she summoned a little counterthrust. She shed her wings and dropped directly in front of the front gate of the junkyard and into a roll. In an instant, she found her feet, ready to fight.

Huh. That's not what I expected.

The gate stood open. Although rust ate away at the metal of the gate and the concertina wire above it, there were no scorch marks or bullet holes and no indications of any attack damage. There were also no wounded or dead gang members on the ground. In fact, there was nothing to raise any concern at all. Discarded beer bottles, joints, and baggies with Dust residue lay strewn about the area. Someone obviously used it, but they had no guard at the front.

Alison extended a shadow blade and crept forward. "I'm here, but I don't see anything. What about you, Tahir?"

"My drones are still about ten minutes out, and there's no satellite in position for imaging," he responded. "I've tried to open a scrying window, but there's odd resistance. I thought you said they didn't have any magicals? By the way, Mason and Drysi are about thirty minutes away.

Hana's doing what you requested and staying at the Brownstone Building."

"The Red Bears don't have any magicals," she commented. "But if some wizard is here and using Ultimate, who knows what he could pull off, especially if it's a more powerful form."

A couple of gunshots sounded in the distance.

"Okay, I hear something. I'll investigate."

She rushed toward the noise, her sword at the ready. The piles of crushed metal filling most of the junkyard formed a maze. She sprinted around a shiny pile and skidded to a stop. Six men lay on the ground in pools of their own blood. They wore the red-and-black bandanas of the Red Bears. Some of the bodies had gaping wounds in their chests. Other poor men had their throats torn out. At least one man's arm had been ripped off.

"What the hell?" she murmured. "It's like an animal went after them."

"It behooves me on behalf of Mason to encourage you to be careful. We don't know the capabilities of Ultimate, especially the purer form."

"Don't worry. You don't need to tell me that." She frowned. "My dad mentioned some weird things, but it wasn't like this."

Another flurry of gunshots nearby spurred her into action.

"I'm on the move," she announced.

Alison rushed forward and leapt upward as she conjured new wings. She ascended for several seconds until she cleared the height of the scrap mountains. More

Red Bears lay scattered behind the piles, many obviously dead, and about a dozen men were penned in by heaps of metal. A man in a torn T-Shirt and jeans advanced on two of the gang members and raised his long, clawed hands. The defenders opened fire, but their tormentor's slight jerks were the only indication that he felt anything. He didn't howl in pain or even offer a muttered protest. Instead, he lunged forward and attacked the closest man.

Alison hissed and thrust her palm out. A blast of light magic struck the clawed man's back. He shrieked in pain this time and rounded on her.

"Get the hell out of here!" she shouted and flung another light bolt. The assassin stumbled away, his chest burned, but the flesh began to grow back within a few seconds. She released another attack, and he hissed as his flesh blackened.

The gang members took their chance and sprinted forward while her strikes suppressed their adversary.

The clawed man growled and hissed. He banged his hand against his chest. "This isn't your business, Brownstone!" His voice was guttural and inhuman. "How dare you interfere."

She raised her blade instead of firing again. "My dad's dealt with Ultimate, but what he saw wasn't nearly as freaky as this." She stepped closer and narrowed her eyes. The man's veins were dark and his eyes solid black." She gritted her teeth. "You're with the Tapestry?"

"What the hell are you talking about, Brownstone?" the man snarled. "I don't need any weak-ass nicknames. I'm Leon Smith, and I'll be the wizard who killed Alison

Brownstone unless you leave right now. I won't harm any innocent people. I'll only kill some gang scum."

Alison crept closer and circled to his side. "You're telling me you're not a Strand or Weaver? You're saying you have nothing to do with the Tapestry?"

"You're afraid." The wizard laughed. His earlier burns had already healed. "Of course you are. Ultimate evens the score. You're not so powerful now, Dark Princess, are you? You're a half-breed freak blessed with a little extra power, and what do you do with it? You could own the town. Instead, you run around playing at being a good little girl."

She studied him intently. Leon's eyes and veins were very similar to what she'd seen with the Tapestry members, but the speech patterns and overall basic appearance were wildly different. Perhaps it was a coincidence.

"A wizard who doesn't use a wand." She shook her head. "I knew Ultimate could enhance things, but that's a whole other level of different."

"Exactly." He licked his lips. "Get on your knees and beg me for my mercy, and I might let you live." He cackled.

"No offense, but have you looked in the mirror? Because you look like a monster."

"I don't care. People fear monsters, and fear is power. Surrender, Brownstone."

Alison shook her head. "Just because you've gone a little strange doesn't mean you can win against me." She pointed at a dead man. "This is pointless. What do you hope to prove? You could have probably killed these guys without Ultimate."

Leon took a few steps forward. "I know. They're vermin

and I'm not afraid of the Eastern Union. Killing them is pointless, but I was told to test it, so here I am. Now that I'm here, though, I have to say I'm really enjoying it."

"Test it? The Ultimate?"

He nodded. "They're going to give me more of it. Seattle's special, Brownstone. We're getting the pure form. There's nothing you can do. We'll own this town soon enough, and you and all the cops will have to come and beg us for mercy."

Talk about delusions of grandeur. Dad said his guys were annoying, too. Whatever. I've had enough.

"Get on your knees and put your hands on your head," she commanded coldly. "You don't have to die, but you'd better not give me a reason to kill you. It'd be one thing if you actually had a beef with the Red Bears, but you're simply murdering people for the fun of it."

"No!" He growled belligerently. "Not for the fun of it. To prove something."

"Oh, yeah, I forgot. Because your *dealer* told you to. All you're proving is that you're a rabid animal." She wrinkled her nose in disgust. "Did you even give them a chance to surrender?"

"No. You don't negotiate with vermin. You exterminate them." He drew a deep, shuddering breath. "And I needed to see my full power. I needed to understand how strong I could become."

"Where did you get the Ultimate?" she demanded. "You'll either die here or go to prison, so you might as well tell me."

"Jealous, Brownstone?" He slid his claws across one

another. "Do you want to taste true power and not your feeble half-breed crap?"

"You're so far beyond testing my patience that it's in another galaxy at this point, asshole. So shut the hell up other than to answer my questions."

Leon scoffed. "So you still think you're better than me? Then suffer." He jerked his arm up and fired a blue bolt from his palm.

The attack struck her head-on and exploded in a shower of sparks and arcing blue energy. She catapulted with a grunt and slammed into a pile of metal, her shields depleted, and pain coursed through her body.

What the hell?

Alison gritted her teeth and summoned another shield, ignoring the pain. She stood. "That's the only strike I'll give you. The only reason I haven't eliminated you yet is because I need that information."

The wizard laughed. "I didn't think I'd need to test it more, but you're here and you're a little harder to kill than some vermin." His head twitched a few times. "The whispers are distracting."

"Whispers? What whispers?"

"You'll never know." He reached into his shredded pocket and withdrew a familiar spiky black crystal.

She hissed in outrage.

Damn it. It is the Tapestry, after all. That might explain why Tahir is having trouble.

"That's a True Core." She frowned. "Did you use a green Core before? Is that why you can regenerate? But why are you so different than the other Strands and Weavers?"

"Strands? Weavers? I don't know what you're talking

about." He tossed the True Core into his mouth and swallowed. His whole body convulsed, and he collapsed and howled in pain.

Okay, that's not what I expected.

His cries ceased after a few seconds. He remained on his back and his convulsions finally settled into subdued twitching.

Alison took the opportunity to layer on a few more shields and rushed forward. She put her blade at his throat as he settled. "You got cocky, and now you're even in a worse position. So you'll answer my questions."

Leon growled defiance. "Screw you."

"What is the Tapestry?" she shouted. "Are you even human? Where are you from?"

"I'm not the Tapestry," the man retorted angrily. "I'm Leon, you bitch!" He jerked an arm up.

She rolled out of the way as he fired another blue bolt, shunted magic into her leg, and kicked his chest. The powerful, enhanced blow launched him several yards and his flight ended when he impacted with a dense pile of cubed metal. He fell forward, his back shredded from the contact, but his wounds were already healing. The wizard stood and snarled.

"Don't you get it, Brownstone?" Leon screamed. "I'm not some Eastern Union trash. I'm not some feeble dark wizard obsessed with you. I've taken Ultimate, and I'm strong. You can't win against me. You've wounded me several times, and I always heal."

Alison scoffed. "Is that what the Tapestry does? Changes people into those Strand drones?" She flung a stun bolt at the wizard. He dropped to one knee but didn't fall.

"Your blood," he murmured. "I'll give them your blood. They'll reward me even more. I'll become even stronger."

She launched two stun bolts. The wizard's body jerked but he stood without difficulty and a sick smile spread slowly across his face.

"Keep in mind," she began, "if you attack me again, I will kill you. I want information from you, but that doesn't mean I'll sit here and let you destroy me."

Leon held his arm out to the side. A crackling blue energy blade appeared.

"You like the swords, Brownstone," he whispered. "I'll kill you with one, then. Won't that be poetic?"

Alison threw her arm out and conjured a shadow crescent. The sharp attack struck her adversary and ripped deep into his body. Blood sprayed everywhere and he staggered back with a growl.

His head twitched several times as the huge laceration began to seal. The new muscle appeared and knitted itself together, and fresh skin began to cover it.

This is ridiculous. This is like Dad-level regeneration.

"Last chance, Leon," she offered. "Where did you get the Ultimate?"

"Maybe she'll let me join her," Leon shouted. "If this is what it means, I want to join her."

"She? Who?" She hadn't seen any female Tapestry members, but the organization might have different factions.

"She's perfection. I understand that now." The man took

a few deep breaths. "Someone like you would never understand."

"You won't escape, Leon. I hope *you* understand that. Not after everything you've done."

"It's time to end you, you arrogant bitch. We don't need Drow royalty in Seattle." He rushed toward her and raised his blue energy sword.

You give me no choice.

Alison spun out of the way of the wizard's clumsy slice. For all his impressive strength and regeneration, his speed was subpar compared to the Strands she'd fought before. He stumbled forward with a grunt, now off-balance. She sliced through his sword arm at the shoulder and the clean cut severed the limb. The blue sword disappeared and its faint buzz faded into silence.

Leon howled and whipped the claws on his remaining arm. Her shields slowed the vicious attack but he forced her back. She swung her blade at the wizard's neck and decapitated him. His body fell and she stepped away to watch and wait.

Will he regenerate?

She stared at the body parts, her breathing heavy. Finally—she wasn't sure how long it was—Tahir broke her concentration.

"I have a drone over you now," he advised her. "There was some interference before, but it just went away. I see you've been busy."

"I only killed the one wizard." She sighed. "He killed the others. I couldn't save all of them, but at least I stopped him from slaughtering everyone."

"Are you all right, A?" Mason asked, worry in his voice.

I wonder how long he's been listening. Maybe he didn't want to break my concentration.

"I'm fine. There was one wizard here, but he'd radically changed. He could do magic without a wand and he was kind of feral." She sighed again, hating all the unanswered questions that crowded in. "And I'm sure the Tapestry is the source of Ultimate."

"What?" he asked.

Hana's recognizable hiss sounded through the comms.

"The wizard ate a True Core right in front of me," Alison muttered.

"And you're sure?" Tahir sounded skeptical. "Maybe it was only a pill you thought looked like a True Core."

"Yeah." She shook her head. "It's not like there are huge numbers of weird spiky crystals and I can confuse one for another."

"But his body's still there," the infomancer observed. "That's not consistent with what we've seen from them before."

"I don't know, but it was definitely a True Core, and some of the side-effects were the same." She scowled as she studied the headless corpse. "But you're right. He didn't act like the Tapestry. I think he's only a normal wizard mutated by the True Core."

"Crap," Mason muttered. "The regular Tapestry guys were annoying enough."

Alison reached a decision. "This is out of control. We need to contact the PDA and let them know that the Tapestry is the source of Ultimate. It was one thing when they simply sent their own guys, but if they're changing locals, that's a completely different type of threat. Worse, if they are what I'm worried they are, it means this isn't simply criminal activity. This is an invasion."

"Are you going to express…all your theories to the authorities?" Tahir probed. "They might find them difficult to believe."

"No. But I won't let the Tapestry overrun Seattle."

CHAPTER NINE

A gent Latherby leaned back in his chair and frowned. "So, to summarize what you've told me, you're currently in possession of some kind of unidentified magical creature that the Tapestry wants, and you believe they are also responsible for Ultimate?"

Alison folded her arms and nodded. She'd wrestled with the mental debate of how much to tell the PDA agent before she settled on basically everything except her theory that the Tapestry might be non-Oriceran aliens. He already knew about the existence of the group from her report after the warehouse battle, but she'd also conveniently left out specific details concerning Omni.

"So, Agent Latherby, my first question for you is easy for me but may be hard for you. However, I need to know because it might cause a problem with my people, and they always come first." She took a deep breath. "What do you intend to do about Omni?"

He pursed his lips and his gaze grew distant. He refocused on her after a few seconds. "For now, nothing."

She blinked. "Nothing?"

"Since the identity of the creature is unclear, it means there is also no clear prohibition of its transfer to Earth or the US and, more to the point, from what you've told me, you didn't bring it here. You simply found it, meaning you're not in violation of any relevant federal magical control laws."

"It's that simple?" She frowned. "Really?"

"No." The agent shook his head. "It's actually hideously complex. The truth is, our laws on this sort of matter are very far behind, but it's difficult to write clear laws about things such as invasive and dangerous species when you have a planet with thousands of intelligent species and everything between. It's why they've focused mainly on identifying specific species and prohibiting them. On a more practical level, I have no wish to agitate you or your employees, and my experiences with your company suggest that if the creature is being contained by you successfully, there's no reason to change the status quo."

Alison released a sigh of relief. "Good, that makes things easier. If you tried to come and take Omni, I think Hana would rip your throat out."

He frowned. "And you're sure she's not under magical control of some sort?"

She shook her head firmly. "The power of cute compels her, but it's all natural—or at least not magical."

"I'll make my formal recommendations on that matter and distribute them to the relevant agencies and partners. I'll also make the Seattle PD aware of things." He ran his hand over his shaved head. "But setting that aside, certain things are now much, much clearer. Disparate lines of evidence are falling into place."

Alison raised an eyebrow. "What evidence?"

"Several different agencies have worked on the Ultimate question, and the investigations have always dead-ended at the mid-level distributors. They've spoken of cryptic and strange distributors, but all these criminals don't seem to have any real understanding of who might actually be trading them their product." Agent Latherby steepled his fingers. "The only thing we've learned is that money is sometimes involved, but payment in kind is increasingly common—especially the blood of magicals, which of course has any number of ritualistic implications."

"What about Alphonse Tatum?" she asked. "Isn't he back in town? Might he be connected?"

"Or so the rumors say, but he's been tracked to several cities where Ultimate hasn't appeared. His interests are consistent with something like Ultimate, but his presence here in Seattle—if he actually is here—might be a coincidence." He shrugged. "The current popular theory among many government agents working on the Ultimate issue is that it was created by a group of rogue Oricerans who are running an op to weaken some of the stronger Earth countries, but I've never been partial to that theory."

"Why? You think the Oricerans wouldn't do that?"

The man shook his head. "No, the Oricerans were fine with all kinds of deceptions and limitations for thousands of years, even aided as they were by magicals from Earth. All documented Ultimate cases are in the United States. It makes no sense to weaken America but not target China or Russia. Both have robust magical populations who could be a lucrative market."

Alison nodded. "And you're sure these Tapestry guys aren't foreign intelligence? That's what you told me before."

"I'm as sure as anyone gets in my line of work." He snorted. "Defending the country against magical threats often introduces a certain amount of uncertainty to any given investigation."

Wait. Does he think they're aliens? He's hinted a few times that he knows the truth about Dad, but he's never outright said it.

"So who do you think they are then if not Oricerans?" she asked.

Agent Latherby shrugged. "Some wizard faction. Not explicitly dark wizards following the ways of the old families but some group attempting to increase their magical power for the same reason such groups always do—because they seek control and domination. Your friend's pet fits into that plan in some manner, but considering Ultimate is altering people, it's a far greater immediate concern."

"The guys I dealt with before all mostly looked alike," she pointed out. "They weren't *identical* but definitely alike, and even the way they talked was weird."

"Many organizations have requirements designed to reinforce uniformity." He pointed to his suit. "Whether dress codes…" He pointed to his head. "Or grooming standards. If they are also some kind of ideological terrorist group or cult, that might explain it. Given their apparent willingness to experiment with magical items that alter people's biology, they are likely highly advanced in life magic techniques. We'll examine the body of the Ultimate user you killed in Tacoma, but don't expect much. Previous autopsies and genetic analyses of Ultimate users in other cities haven't turned up anything of note other than obvious magical alteration, but if the form of Ultimate being used in this area is different, we might find something."

Forced appearance changes? Weird ranks? I'd half-convinced myself they were aliens, but he's right. They might simply be a weird terrorist group trying to get stronger. New Veil members are weird and spout gibberish, too, and they don't use something like True Cores.

Maybe they've all used their magic too much and it's warped their minds as much as their bodies.

Agent Latherby frowned. "While I can't offer you a formal assignment at this time, I am prepared to use some of my discretionary accounts to fund your continued investigation into the Tapestry, particularly as it applies to the Ultimate issue."

"Really?" Alison shrugged. "I thought you would say the government would handle it from here."

"I wish I could say that. The problem is there are several different agencies jockeying for position on all matters of Ultimate, including the PDA, FBI, and DEA, not to mention the local police." He shrugged again. "Inter-agency cooperation often goes out the window when a new threat first arises. Each agency thinks they can score points, as it were, if they deal with the threat, and it takes some time to settle into proper cooperation. This isn't to say that our various agencies don't investigate and share intelligence, but that the lack of a coordinated joint task force results in inefficiencies. Perhaps if we'd worked together more effectively, we would have been more prepared for Ultimate coming to Seattle." He pointed at her. "But you have your own connections and ways to find information."

She nodded. "I do, although some of them are awfully skittish about the authorities being involved."

"If it makes any difference—at least as far as the local PDA are concerned—I'd like you to focus on doing whatever you can to track the Ultimate distributors. Individual users are unstable and a concern, but they're also nothing Seattle AET can't handle. I'll pass along the information you've shared with me, but I suspect it'll take weeks for the PDA and the other agencies to properly parse and assimilate it into our investigations." Agent Latherby gestured toward his computer on the side of his desk. "I've already looked into the Tapestry once you told me about them, and I've found basically nothing. It's like they don't exist, but that's consistent with some of the passive magic you described. That makes them even more dangerous, especially if they do harbor terrorist intent, but the problem is that the government is always fighting the last war. With limited resources, it can be hard to justify investigations into a group like this without being able to clearly articulate the threat."

Alison frowned. "A weird group of guys distributing Ultimate isn't enough of a threat?"

"I hope it will be, but the wheels of justice often turn

slowly." He folded his hands in front of him. "For now, thank you for your trust in me. Perhaps, if we put pressure on the Tapestry from multiple directions, they'll slip up." He extended his hand.

She shook it. "Thanks for all your help, Agent Latherby."

CHAPTER TEN

The next morning, Alison sat in her office and skimmed the news on her phone until Ava knocked lightly on the half-open door.

She looked up and smiled. "What is it?"

Her assistant frowned. "You have a rather unusual visitor. I would have used the intercom, but I think you deserve to see him to experience the same reaction I did."

Immediately, her smile faded. "Who is it?"

Wait. Maybe it's nothing bad. A surprise visit by Dad?

Ava opened the door wider and gestured inside. Vincent stood in the hallway in a green suit with silver chains, a slight smirk on his face although dark bags hung under his eyes and robbed his expression of some of his usual confidence.

She sighed and nodded to Ava. "I half-expected this after yesterday. Don't worry. I have the time to talk to him now."

"Should I get his men refreshments?" The assistant's gaze cut toward the main lobby. "All of them?"

"You brought your entire army?" She frowned at him. "Why?"

He shrugged. "What did you expect me to do? It's not like this place is safe. It's been attacked before." He stepped inside the office and looked around. "There's not much in here. Somehow, I'm not surprised. For someone as rich as you, you sure don't know how to show it off properly."

Alison turned to Ava. "Go ahead and get them something. This might take a few minutes."

The woman nodded politely. She cast a disdainful glare at Vincent before she closed the door behind her.

"Some of us don't care about showing wealth off." She gestured to the empty seat in front of her desk. "That said, this is a weird day. I never thought you would come to me instead of the other way around."

Vincent sat with a shrug. "Life's always changing, and that necessitates certain actions at certain times. A man who doesn't adapt is a man who gets left behind."

"And coming here is you adapting? I assume this is about the Tacoma incident?"

He nodded. "I knew I needed to talk to you after what I heard, and I thought why waste time to drag you down to the True Portal? Besides, I wanted to see this place. You're the Dark Princess, and I haven't been in your palace yet." He bowed over his arm with a smirk. "Consider this my supplication."

She rolled her eyes. "Fair enough. Now, what have you heard? If you came here, it must have been something that upset you."

He gestured vaguely in a show of indifference. "Upset is a strong word. Let's simply say it's left me concerned. I've heard that the government's all over Ultimate now and that they think it has something to do with some group called the Tapestry." He frowned at her. "I thought we had a mutual understanding but apparently, I was wrong."

"Are you seriously here to bitch that I told the government a few things after I eliminated an out-of-control Ultimate user?" She snorted. "You're the one who told me you didn't like Ultimate. You also said you didn't care if the authorities got involved after the fact. Did you really think I would blow the cops and PDA off entirely? Even I have to explain to people why I cut a man's head off and why I was present at a scene with dozens of dead bodies." She fixed him with a hard look. "And I might withhold information from the cops and PDA, but I won't lie to them and make trouble for myself in the future."

"You've made quite a few assumptions." Vincent shook his finger and clucked his tongue.

"Then clarify for me where I've gone wrong. Because right now, I'm fairly agitated about this Ultimate situation for reasons that have nothing to do with you, so I find it hard to care about what you think."

"You see, you telling the cops after the fact isn't what has me concerned. It was inevitable eventually, and I knew that. I mostly wanted to slow you down and make sure you didn't point too many mobsters at me along the way." He smiled benignly. "But you're right. I wanted you to not get the cops involved ahead of time, and you did that, but what I'm more interested in is this Tapestry because you didn't mention them to me before. I told you about Tatum and now, I find out second-hand that I might have been wrong, yet you didn't even hint about that to me."

Is that what this is all about? His feelings being hurt? Is this only about his pride?

Alison scoffed. "You're an information broker. You know that sometimes, it's best to keep the distribution of information limited because it has value. You didn't need to know about the Tapestry before now. I wasn't aware until the Tacoma incident that they might be linked to Ultimate, and they were a separate problem I was handling with the assistance of some PDA contacts." She leaned forward and tried her best to copy Vincent's standard-issue slimy smile. "Not only that, I didn't tell you about the Tapestry because I intended to wipe them out and the information would have been stale. I'll give you a *freebie*, though. Tatum might not even be involved with Ultimate. According to my PDA contact, it's probably a coincidence that he's here."

The man laughed scornfully. "Some PDA agent with a stick up his ass doesn't know shit about this kind of thing. Why do you think they need you to clean up after them? The idiots let a dark wizard double-agent run free for how long?" He slammed his fist on her desk. "Some dumb-ass PDA agent doesn't have the kind of instincts I do. The government doesn't know shit and can't stop anything." His nostrils flared.

Her gaze dipped to his reddened fist and returned to his face. "What the hell is going on with you? This isn't like you at all, and I don't think this is only because there's no one around to witness what is going on."

A smirk erased the frown that had reappeared on his face. "What do you mean? I'm fine. Can't a man be a little passionate about the failings of the government?

"No, you're not fine. You've been off since I saw you the other day, and you're traveling around with a Jericho Cartwright-sized entourage. Are you that afraid of Tatum? Does he have some particular reason to target you?"

"Fuck Tatum," Vincent retorted. "I'm sure you'll deal with him soon enough, one way or another, and this has nothing to do with him." His smirk faded, and his shoulders slumped. "Do you know why I do what I do?"

"To make money, I assume."

"You're damned right," he snapped. "I'm not here to save the day like you, Dark Princess. I'm here to make money off everyone I can. Sometimes, that means I help people dedicated to helping others, and sometimes, it means I help nastier people. That's how I keep myself in my nice clothes and jewelry."

She nodded. "I sense a but coming."

"I told you before, there's a certain stability that's required in the city for people of my trade." He stared at the desk. "And when things get out of hand, I can't let that slide, which means sometimes, I help your type more than I should."

"I won't disagree with that. What does any of this have to do with why you're afraid of your own shadow?"

His jaw tightened and he raised his head slowly, his gaze full of fire. "I'm not afraid of you. Let me make that damned clear."

Alison shrugged. "You've not given me a reason to want to convince you otherwise. Until you do, you have no reason to be afraid of me, but you're obviously afraid of someone."

"One damned time," he muttered. "One damned time, I

forgot that it should be about money and my own position. One time, I let some stupid ideas of morality screw me over."

"What are you talking about?"

Vincent took a deep breath. "It was about five years back. I wasn't as established as I am now, but I was an up-and-comer in the game. People knew me, and I was building some solid relationships. Because of those, I heard all kinds of things, including one day when I landed some nice, juicy information that might have been worth a considerable amount to some bounty hunters. I should have found some to sell it to."

"What information was this?"

"Have you ever heard about the Rizal Massacre?"

She frowned. "I vaguely remember reading about that. The family of a governor in the Philippines was killed, including his wife and children. He committed suicide shortly after. They said it might have had something to do with local corruption. Magical organized crime or something. I don't remember much after that."

"Yeah, local corruption." He shook his head. "The governor had stumbled across some shit he didn't need to know about, and he was assassinated by a trio of American magical hitmen hired by political rivals. The hitman used twisted magic to kill the family, but the suicide was a bonus. I happened to stumble on a few pieces of evidence about the hit because those three hitmen were based out of Seattle, and I thought, you know, why not help the poor bastard get some revenge from the afterlife? Killing kids?"

He shrugged. "Where's the profit in that, right? That's what I thought. So I passed my info onto the PDA instead of some bounty hunter who could have cut me in for a share. I thought I was doing the right thing. The PDA did a raid and caught the bastards." He chuckled darkly. "They were supposed to keep my name out of it but somehow, it leaked. The hitmen swore they would come for me, but I didn't sweat it at first." He fingered one of his chains. "I'm not saying I wasn't a little spooked, but they were extradited to the Philippines, and then they were executed. That calmed me. It was a little while after the massacre, by the way, so it didn't get much attention in the news."

Alison frowned and thought about what he'd said. "That sounds about right based on my recollection. I didn't realize you were involved. They might have leaked your name, but it wasn't a household name."

"It didn't need to be a household name. It only needed to be out in the underworld." He hissed with frustration. "I found out last week that only one of them was actually executed." He laughed, a desperate quality underlying it. "The other two swapped out two other poor bastards for them. I guess they've been laying low and waiting. I didn't think that much about it until two of my boys ended up with their throat slits and 'Remember Rizal' written in their blood beside them." He shook his head. "This is what happens when you don't focus only on the money. I've never let myself have an attack of conscience since."

"Why not go to the cops or the PDA?" she asked.

Vincent snorted. "What good are they? They should have followed up and made sure those guys were dead, and they shouldn't have leaked my damned name. Even without the damned hitmen planning their revenge, it hurt me for years. People thought I was a police snitch, and it took considerable time and effort to prove I wasn't. But now, they're back and they've painted a target on me." He ruffled his hair. "I've tried to play it cool, but there's not much profit in being an information broker if you have to bring twelve guys with you everywhere. Now, we have this Ultimate shit and Tatum and this Tapestry, too. Chaos. It's bad for business."

Alison nodded slowly. "You know what the easiest solution would have been?"

"To never help the damned PDA to begin with?" He shrugged. "Worthless government idiots."

"To ask me for help. I know we're not friends, but I told you before, you're useful. Besides that, it's not exactly like I'm a fan of murderous hitmen, especially ones who are already supposed to be dead for their crimes."

He gaped at her. "Wait. What are you saying?"

"I'm going to save your life, Vincent," she explained with a smirk. "And you're going to owe me one. This will be easy."

"Easy?" He stared at her, his expression still caught in a frown but with a hint of hope in his eyes.

She shrugged. "Yeah, easy. You're good at spreading the word, so you'll give the hitmen exactly what they want."

"And what's that?" he asked warily.

"Your location at a time when you have minimal guards." She smiled.

CHAPTER ELEVEN

Mirela closed the door of the luxury hotel suite and paused, her head tilted as she stilled. She turned slowly. A few strands of stray light slipped in through the bottom of the closed curtains, a small sliver of evidence of the bright glory of downtown Seattle. The light provided the barest illumination of the frosted glass table in the dining nook and the three-piece sectional sofa in the living room arrayed around a low, dark table.

The intrusion wards hadn't been tripped, but something felt off. She could sense that someone or something was watching her. Eagerness, rather than fear, filled her. It would be easy enough to leave the hotel, and another kill would remove an enemy and provide more blood for her leader's experiments.

Casually, she slid her glove off. There was no reason to dirty a perfectly good glove. Light glinted off the crystals that covered her hand.

She looked around her before she focused to stare at

her empty couch. A faint humanoid haze stood in front of it and dark, angry colors flowed across it.

The intruder deserved some respect. She would grant them that much. Whoever he or she was, they had managed to enter without tripping her wards and used invisibility magic that would have rendered them hidden to most witches who hadn't been enhanced with her recent gifts. It would be a shame to have to kill such a talented person, but she also couldn't let them go.

"The only reason you're not yet dead is because I wish to confirm my target," Mirela announced calmly. "Suite, lights on."

The bright, warm lights flicked on in response to her voice command. The vague haze remained rigidly in place.

"I have little patience for games." She took a few steps toward the couch. "Show yourself, or you will force me to kill you immediately. This doesn't worry me, but it will cause me slight inconvenience." She raised a hand. "But if you reveal yourself, some negotiation is possible."

It might be unlikely but not impossible.

The form shimmered for a moment and coalesced into a dark-haired, olive-skinned man in an expensive dark-blue suit and bow tie. A wand hung loosely in his fingers.

Mirela bowed her head and jerked her hand down. "Alphonse, I'm sorry. I didn't know it was you."

The wizard tucked his wand into a holster inside his jacket, a faint smile on his face. "There is no need for apologies, Mirela. I would have been disappointed if you'd reacted any other way. All hypotheses are useless until they're tested, and that's what this was—a test of sorts."

"A test?"

Alphonse nodded. "The experiments are proceeding well, but there are still many uncertainties." He sighed. "This means the changes continue to be difficult to anticipate, let alone direct. While this doesn't negate my overall progress, it has forced me to rely on more creative thinking in this matter."

She nodded although she didn't really understand, but it didn't matter. There was no need to understand all his plans or thoughts. She simply needed to execute his orders.

He walked around the couch and set his hand on the back. "When you described some recent incidents to me in a report, it set me to thinking about possibilities. Then I realized I've been far too focused on certain key attributes and power levels and missed other opportunities." He shook his head, a disappointed look on his face. "And that means I missed certain things that were obvious in retrospect."

"Alphonse?" Mirela frowned in bewilderment and honestly didn't care if she looked as lost as she felt.

"You just demonstrated an example. Just now, how did you sense I was there? I'd provided enough background magic through other means that you shouldn't have been able to detect me from that alone, but you clearly knew my exact location."

She shook her head. "I believe I could see your aura."

"Interesting." He ran his tongue along the inside his cheek. "Interesting indeed. When did this start? It wasn't in your last report."

"You told me to only send reports at the designated time."

Alphonse nodded. "And so you should. It's only by

proceeding and operating with caution that I've been able to get this far. I'm not angry, Mirela. I'm only curious."

"It started after I consumed the True Core a customer refused." She looked down. "I apologize for my impertinence."

"I told you that would be our preferred plan in refusals. The modified True Cores are too unstable once you add the priming potion to them." He sighed and frustration crept onto his face. "That's yet another failure on my part, but it doesn't matter. I would prefer you use them rather than let them go to waste, but I do have concerns."

"Of course."

He reached into a pocket and removed a small vial containing a black liquid. He offered it to her. "Remember, you need to be cautious. If I'm not present to monitor the experiments and provide potential buffer potions, difficulties may occur. The True Cores, after all, were never intended for the use we've put them to."

Mirela nodded. "I understand." She accepted the potion, reverence in her eyes.

"Make sure you drink at least one drop of this added to a glass of water a day. Although I value your loyalty and usefulness as an aide, please always remember that your stability is unusual and by no means assured, even with the buffer potions. I understand that you desire further enhancement but let us use the expendable flesh and souls of Seattle to take the main risks."

Alphonse pulled his wand out and murmured a quick spell. A briefcase winked into existence on top of the living room table.

She stared at it, her eyes wide. "Is that what I think

it is?"

He walked over, opened it, and gestured to the contents. Two dozen True Cores of varying colors lay nestled inside a soft gray foam liner.

Mirela's breath caught. "I thought you said there would be no more for a while. You told me the Tapestry were beginning to doubt you."

"They are, but the beginnings of doubt are not the same thing as ceasing aid." He smiled. "I was able to convince the Weaver of the utility of my newer batch of experiments. They understand that they need me as much as I need them. They have no one in their group who could even begin to provide the kind of results I have."

She scowled. "I don't trust the Tapestry. Their plans aren't your plans, Alphonse. They might even attempt to dispose of you when they have finished using you. I've heard their name increasingly as of late, including among the PDA. They are becoming too aggressive for their own good, and that means they'll be confronted, and when they are, they'll attempt to betray you."

"Of course they will." He remained calm and unperturbed. "I would almost be disappointed if they didn't attempt such a thing, but it doesn't matter."

"How can it not matter?" Her hand curled into a first.

"Because for now, I only need them to keep supplying True Cores. Whatever they're doing and whomever else they're doing it to doesn't concern me. Even with some of my concerns about lack of direction, I believe we're close— very close." Alphonse chuckled. "Besides, I'm taking as much advantage of them. They think they'll gain a new, more powerful army to supplement their forces, one they can control, and I know they think I'm not aware of exactly how much the True Cores affect the mind to benefit them."

He pointed at the vial of black liquid. "But I already know how to stop that. I'll use their magic and supplies to create a better strain of magical human but not one beholden to whatever bizarre ideology is motivating their group." He sniffed disdainfully. "It's clear that whatever else they possess, they lack creativity. In that sense, they are failures, and that's why they're forced to rely on outsiders like me. I don't know if they're from Earth or Oriceran, and I don't really care. Once I've perfected the enhancement, we will form a loyal group of our own and destroy the Tapestry if necessary."

"And what if they come for you?" she asked. "You have not yet enhanced yourself, Alphonse."

"I will once I've finished eliminating all unwanted side-effects." He looked down, his gaze distant with thought. "Your service in this regard is appreciated." He walked out of the living room toward the kitchen. "You're helping me lead magicals into the future."

Mirela trailed after him. "Thank you, Alphonse."

He stopped in front of the silver-gray refrigerator and opened it after a brief moment of hesitation. Alphonse smiled at the test tube racks filling all shelves. They held vials of blood sourced from all intelligent species and identified by hand-written labels around the middle of each tube. These included wizards, witches, Light Elves, Gray Elves, gnomes, dwarves, and Nichts, among others.

"Were you able to gather all the necessary types?" He gestured to the blood.

"Yes, Alphonse. There are fourteen species represented

in this collection." She bowed her head.

"Excellent! There are so few cities where we could easily achieve that on Earth. I had hoped to go to Los Angeles to complete this task, but it's too much of a risk with James Brownstone there. And besides, with the Tapestry showing more interest in Seattle, it's made our plans align for easier logistics." He gestured toward the closed window and the city outside. "It's as if destiny is guiding my hand."

Mirela looked away. "Some deaths were necessary to acquire the quantity needed, but I've made sure to cover our tracks, even beyond my normal shroud. The number of deaths has increased since my last report."

"I trust your judgment." Alphonse waved a hand dismissively. "And the fight for the future always costs lives. I can't be bothered to mourn an inevitability we've simply accelerated, especially among expendable flesh." He sighed. "I've made mistakes these last few years, such as wasting the Tears of Eternal Lament on Raven, but these experiments will be the culmination of so many efforts." He closed the refrigerator. "And I will be able to achieve my goal—a perfect new race of magical, something crafted by the directed hand of an Earth wizard, immortal and powerful." He shrugged. "There are billions of lives on Earth and Oriceran. Most are unnecessary, and that will become even more so once I achieve my goal. They are redundant and take up space, and they'll understand that very soon, once we no longer have to fear their numbers."

She nodded. "Still, I think you shouldn't spend so much time alone. There are other risks as well. Threats other than the Tapestry."

"Such as?"

"Alison Brownstone intervened in a recent True Core test." She frowned. "There are other rumors of her interest in Ultimate. She could present a threat."

Alphonse sighed. "She is a troublesome girl, just as her father is troublesome. His disruptions in Las Vegas delayed my experiments, but the solution here is simple because you've been far more careful than my other agents."

"What solution?" She stared at him, her brow creased in confusion.

"We've no current reason to confront her, and we will give her no reason. We're close now. So very close." He shrugged. "Between my wards and your mutations, she won't be able to track either of us directly and I've already disposed of my most troublesome agents in most other locations. If we continue to handle ourselves with discretion, it won't be a problem. I'm willing to admit we've been too aggressive in the past, but the situation is different now, and we will find success, even with the attention of Alison Brownstone."

Mirela nodded. "And in cases of refusal? Should I cease disposing of such people?"

"Follow the same protocol as always. Kill them and dispose of the body. I have no use for test subjects who won't cooperate with my experiments and who might lead my enemies to me." He scowled. "Everyone in this city is so inconsiderate, considering what I'm attempting to achieve. I will continue to push forward on this to reach my goals. No one will stop me, not Alison Brownstone and not the Tapestry."

CHAPTER TWELVE

Here goes attempt number three, Alison thought.

She grinned when she realized that anyone watching the roof of the hardware store would be disturbed by her splashing in the puddles and the lack of an obvious source. A considerable number of these pools remained after the heavy, cold rain the night before, and she was currently invisible as she made her way through the water to the edge overlooking the street. She stopped there and peered across the road at the steakhouse she had rented and filled with Brownstone employees. They all sat inside having a merry meal, their guns and anti-magic deflectors strapped under the table for easy access.

The earlier PR job and the unexpected robber had given her an idea. Why not set a trap along similar lines for would-be assassins? Technically, protecting Vincent was costing her as she fronted all the extensive costs for personnel, locations, and supplies. That was unfortunate but having an information broker who owed her his life would provide long-term dividends in a city like Seattle.

The more people I help, the more people who will trust and help me and the safer I can make the city.

Vincent sat near a front window and carved idly into a steak. Only two of his personal guards were with him. He gesticulated while he laughed at his own joke. He even helped to bait the trap by wearing an atrocious neon-green suit and a mixture of gold and silver chains. His taste remained in question because he defended the outfit even while he admitted it made him stand out. But Alison wasn't there to stop him dressing like a sleazy music producer. She was there to save him from two hitmen.

These guys can't be that tough. They were afraid to touch him when he had his full team of guards. They're probably better at a surprise ambush than in a straight-up fight. That means we have the advantage.

She looked up and down the street. A few cars cruised the wet roads. Gray clouds choked the sky, but only the occasional light mist reached the ground.

"How long will we keep trying this, A?" Mason asked over the comms. "It's been two days and six meals. I don't think these hitmen are listening to the rumors, and as fun as hanging around waiting for them is, I'm beginning to think there has to be a better way to handle this."

Alison frowned, although being alone and with the invisibility spell in place, no one could see it. Boredom raised a philosophical question about its very existence which she pondered briefly before she focused on the discussion at hand. Mason wasn't wrong in his basic assessment.

"I thought these guys would be a little more eager," she replied. She wasn't worried about keeping her voice down as she had layered a sound-absorbing bubble around her mouth. "Tahir, how are you two doing?"

"We're monitoring all drones and cameras, but thus far, we don't see anything suspicious," the infomancer reported. "Sonya thought she spotted something, but it was only a cat coming out of a garbage can."

"Damn." She shook her head. "I understand that they might not make a move when Vincent had a full security team, but it looks like he only has a couple of guys now, and it did yesterday afternoon, too."

"They might be watching and recognize our people," Drysi suggested. "We could keep doing this for weeks or months and nothing might happen. Not all jobs can be tidy."

"I'm fine with waiting longer," Hana murmured. "This steak is delicious. And the fish was, too."

The witch scoffed. "Just because you're a bloody fox and can't turn invisible you get to stay inside."

"I think it's because I'm brilliant, sexy, and fierce too," the other woman replied with a snicker. "And I have an exceptional disguise."

"I don't think a hat and a wig are that brilliant," Alison countered with a chuckle. At least someone was enjoying themselves.

"Why did I end up on alley duty for every place?" Drysi muttered something in Welsh. Her boss didn't need to understand the language to know that whatever she had said was foul.

"Roof duty isn't that much fun either," she pointed out. "They need better drainage up here." She looked down. The weight of her feet displaced the water and made it obvious that someone stood there. She stepped out of the puddle. Small mistakes might tip the hitmen off.

"I understand why we're helping him," Mason stated, "but we have all our attention focused on protecting Vincent now while the Tapestry and Ultimate are still out there."

"I know," she replied. "All the cops and feds are looking into those as well, so that should at least give us some cover. Yes, we're good at investigation, but that doesn't mean we'll be able to find out more than them, and even then, we'll need Vincent's help. He's our best source for more information about Tapestry or Ultimate." She sighed. "Besides, we need to give the plan a chance to work because I don't have a brilliant solution to finding two magical hitmen in a huge city otherwise." She shook her head. "Jerry, how are things inside?"

"Same as ever," he replied. "Everyone's enjoying their meal but there's nothing suspicious. The staff are all the same people we vetted."

"Okay, we'll hold positions for a half-hour more. By that point, Vincent won't be able to sell staying there any longer. Damn. Another waste of time."

And I thought it would work. So much for my clever trick.

Forty-five minutes later, Mason, Alison, and Drysi followed Vincent's Lexus in a disguised Brownstone Security armored SUV. Hana lingered in the restaurant with most of the remaining employees. Having dozens of people leave at virtually the same time in the middle of the day would be too suspicious if anyone was watching. They'd gone through the trouble of carefully staggered entry to the place to throw off initial suspicion.

Mason frowned and he muttered something under his breath.

Alison glanced at him. "Is something wrong?"

"What if he's lying, A?" His hands tightened around the wheel. "What if this whole thing is only him yanking your chain? That would explain why we haven't run into any hitmen."

Drysi chuckled from the seat behind him. "That would be bloody brilliant." She shrugged when he looked over his shoulder to glare at her.

"I checked with Agent Latherby. He did confirm Vincent's story of about five years ago, but they weren't aware of any murders."

"What? Then he is lying."

"I asked Vincent, and he told me he had the bodies taken care of so as to not involve the authorities right away," she explained. "He did leave out the part where he was offered relocation by the government. That's another thing Agent Latherby confirmed."

Drysi looked surprised. "Then he could have been safe."

"Or he thought it would cramp his style."

"It's more evidence against him." Mason shook his head. "He's spinning you up. It's a power play. We'll run around for a couple of weeks protecting him from shadows, and then he'll claim he heard they left town and he can sit back, smug in the knowledge that he had the Dark Princess as a bodyguard and he didn't even have to pay her. He'll probably even tell people that."

"I doubt it. That kind of plan isn't really his style, and Vincent does have a code of sorts. Accurate information is his life. Feeding me a line and wasting my time are too much risk with nothing valuable to gain. Even if he doesn't believe I would kick his ass, he risks me shutting him out."

Mason grunted. "I'm not so sure this is a good idea even if these hitmen are in town."

"Aren't you now?" Drysi glanced at Alison in the rearview mirror, a questioning look in her eyes.

He's only trying to protect me. I understand that, even if it is frustrating.

"Yes." He frowned. "The guy's a piece of trash, and I don't buy into this whole neutral info broker thing. He helps Alison, sure, but he does that for money. He might not like Tatum, but he has no problem providing info to most criminals in Seattle. He's probably made our job harder in the past by dealing information."

Alison thought that over for a few seconds. "I'm not saying that Vincent's a particularly good man, but he is a useful man. Not only that but if there's ever a time I would help him, you must know it would be against the men he actually helped capture because he was genuinely disgusted. Besides, it sends a message."

"A message?"

The Welsh witch snickered. "You've always been a good little boy, Mason, so you don't get it."

"Get what?" he asked.

"I'm in this car with you instead of dead," she explained and gestured vaguely behind them. "Hana's in that restaurant. Both of us are people who targeted Alison in the past.

Tahir was a bloody bastard to her when they first met if everything I've heard is right."

Alison grimaced. "I'm glad he's found new ways to feed his desire to challenge others that involve less chance of someone dying."

Drysi smiled. "The point is that Alison might be the Dark Princess, but she's not some bloody ruthless bitch, which is why she has so many people willing to help her, even in the underworld."

Mason frowned, not convinced. "Just because she helped a few people turn their lives around doesn't mean she can help everyone. Some people are simply scum." He raised a hand to point to the Lexus several cars ahead. "And Vincent himself said the lesson he took from the Rizal incident was to not care about things that don't make him money."

"I'm not claiming I can make Vincent a nice guy who cares about innocent people," Alison clarified. "But he is, at the minimum, a useful man who isn't a completely amoral piece of garbage. It might only be because he cares about keeping the city stable, but that's preferable to someone who doesn't care at all about who is in town and who might get hurt. I've spent considerable time and effort cultivating different contacts in this city. Spending a week or two guarding one isn't the end of the world, especially when we don't have any immediate leads on either Ultimate or the Tapestry." She frowned. "We might need to come up with a different plan, though. The restaurant idea might not work."

"Or it might have," Tahir interjected.

Her heart rate accelerated. "What are you talking about?"

"Sonya and I have kept our drones rather high, but someone else is now obviously following Vincent's Lexus with a drone. I thought it might be coincidental, but when I attempted to probe it using my own as a relay, it was magically shielded." He snorted. "I could overwhelm it if you want, but that would make our involvement obvious."

"No, leave it alone." She grinned. "If it is them, we need them to believe they have the advantage."

Drysi unzipped her jacket and tapped on the hilt of one her enchanted throwing knives. "Maybe they saw through all the men we had at the restaurant, after all. If it were me tracking someone in this situation…" She narrowed her eyes. "They've already worked his nerves by killing his other men. He knows they've targeted him, which means the next step is simply to kill him."

"Yeah, so?" Mason asked. "We know all that."

"If they have a drone tailing the vehicle, there's a good chance they'll attack the vehicle," she pointed out.

Alison nodded. "I agree. Vincent has a decent shield spell on it in addition to armor. These men must know his general capabilities."

The wizard frowned. "They'll cut him off somewhere. If it becomes a mobility game, it ups the risk factor too much. Maybe we should lean into it. Have him stop somewhere to bait them."

"I don't want to risk any random people." She frowned. "We should have set up a fake restaurant somewhere closer to an abandoned mall or something rather than an actual place."

Drysi shook her head. "If they didn't buy it with what we had, they wouldn't have believed a pop-up."

"The route we plotted earlier gives us thirty minutes on the road. Should we simply wait it out?"

Mason turned at an intersection to keep Vincent's car in sight. "We're not using the same route as before, so that means we probably don't have to worry about mines. The fact that they have the drone on him means they'll probably attack sooner rather than later. Thirty minutes is most likely our absolute limit."

"Wait for the bastards to make their move, then," Drysi suggested.

"I agree." Alison took a deep breath and nodded. "I'll call Vincent and let him know the situation." She reached for her phone as it rang and blinked in surprise, but it wasn't Vincent. The caller ID informed her it was Ruby Sumner, Rasila's human guise.

She sighed. If she didn't answer, the other Drow princess might take it as some kind of slight. Their relationship remained confused and uncertain.

"Hello, *Ruby*," Alison answered. "I'd love to chat, but I'm kind of in the middle of something important."

"Oh, Alison," Rasila replied with a hint of amusement. "You're always in the middle of something important."

"Seriously," she snapped. "I can't talk about this right now. I'll call you later."

"I see." The woman chuckled. "Perhaps I'll stop and see you soon."

"No, you really shouldn't."

"Very well, then. I did have a few things I wanted to discuss, but if you're ever so busy, we can discuss it at a more opportune time." Rasila sounded more amused than annoyed. "There's merely someone I want you to meet."

"Sure, but not right now. Okay?"

"I see. I'll explain your difficulties."

She groaned and ended the call. "When it rains, it pours."

CHAPTER THIRTEEN

"The drone pulled away," Tahir reported a few minutes later. "Rather abruptly." Faint tension underlined his voice, unusual for the infomancer.

Alison took a deep breath. "They're about to make their move, but what it is?"

Mason tapped the brakes as the Lexus and several vehicles ahead slowed. An eight-wheeler had overturned and blocked the road. "I think they've already made their move." He looked into his rearview mirror. "We're boxed in here by traffic and the wreck."

She threw her door open, scrambled out, and layered a few shields over herself before pooling magic in her legs. "Drysi, Mason, try to evacuate as many people as you can away from the area." She released the magic, launched upward, and extended her wings to raise herself above the traffic. Her gaze scanned the lines of cars in search of the assassins.

Drysi and Mason rushed in opposite directions to wave

their arms, bang on the windows of vehicles, and gesture for people to flee.

Alison ground her teeth. She needed to find the enemy. They weren't terrorists but vengeful hitmen, and Vincent was their target. The men needed to be close.

Massive waves of magic passed through her. Bile rose in the back of her throat.

She gasped. "What the hell was that? Did you feel that?"

"Yeah," Drysi replied over the comms.

"Me too," Mason added.

"Alison, there's a major thermal build-up in the over-turned truck," Tahir reported.

"Oh no." She released her wings and landed in front of Vincent's Lexus to point away from the truck. "Run!" she yelled.

Asphalt slabs erupted from the ground and knocked her away. She grunted and lurched to her feet. The slabs formed a cage around the Lexus to enclose the information broker and his men. For a few seconds, she thought he had done it to protect himself before she realized that someone else nearby had sprung the trap.

They're here. I understand now. They couldn't simply kill him—they want him to suffer first. But damn it, why will they take innocent people with them?

Alison raised her hands and forced magic into a broad, shimmering dome over the truck. Dark lines and speckles spread over the barrier.

I can do this. All I have to do is focus. Their arrogance will give me a chance.

She took several deep breaths as she continued to

strengthen the dome but the huge size strained even her powerful magical reserves.

"A, what are you trying to do?" Mason shouted over the comms.

"Keep running," she shouted. "I have to contain the explosion. There are still too many people nearby, let alone if these buildings go down. Tahir, contact the cops and get some air ambulances on their way."

"From what I can feel, even you wouldn't be able to contain it," Mason replied. "Just run. There's nothing we can do."

"If I can at least lower the impact, that's all I need to do." She continued to feed more energy into the dome. "I won't run, not when so many people could get hurt."

"Bloody hell!" Drysi called over the comms. "I'm on my way back. We can at least feed the dome."

"Good idea," he replied.

Several more pulses of magic passed through her and the intensity churned her stomach. The hitmen couldn't have this sort of power. Even if she charged her strongest attack, it wouldn't approach this level.

An artifact? Maybe even something they got from our not so friendly neighborhood smugglers before we took them out.

Alison closed her eyes and continued to push every ounce of magic she could into the barrier.

You damned bastards. Was killing Vincent so important that you had to hurt all these other people?

"A portal is opening on top of the building to your left," Tahir reported.

"Damn it," Mason muttered. "A, Drysi and I will deal

with them. If you won't run, stay on the dome. Wait—what the hell?"

She held her breath and glanced to her side.

Yeah. This is definitely a what the hell moment.

Rasila descended slowly with her shadow wings extended. A half-dozen other Drow leapt off the building and landed with ease. Another tall muscular Drow woman in close-fitting black armor flew down behind them. The armor, despite being shaped to her body, presented the hard, rigid texture of obsidian. A black sword rested in a sheath at her side.

"Huh?" Alison muttered.

Rasila laughed and raised her hands to add magic to the dome. The other Drow did the same, including the swordswoman. The concentrated pressure of the combined magic almost overwhelmed Alison as much as the magic from the truck.

"We're almost there, A," Mason shouted.

Her stomach lurched as a blue-white explosion mushroomed from the back of the truck and consumed it in a blinding flash. The massive thrust of energy pounded against the barrier. She fell to one knee and her vision swam for a few seconds as the light of the explosion faded and left a dense cloud of debris and a huge crater. She forced herself to her feet. The other Drow lowered their hands, and the swordswoman looked at Rasila with a thin frown. She drew her sword.

What now?

The Drow princess snickered. "I told you she was probably doing something pointlessly sacrificial, Miar. You two are so drearily similar in many ways."

Alison blinked a few times. "Miar? As in Miar, the Princess of the Soul Shadow?"

The Drow touched the flat of her blade to her forehead. "It's my pleasure to meet you, Princess of the Shadow Forged. This is not the situation in which I expected to do so, but it does give me a chance to see your true capabilities."

Drysi and Mason slowed as they approached the group. Both held wands and uneasy expressions had settled on their faces. They looked from the gathered Drow to Alison.

"Is everything okay, A?" Mason scowled at Miar's sword.

"I think so." She grimaced and rushed toward Vincent's stone prison. "I think we did some kind of triple princess save, but I have a feeling this isn't over."

"Excellent," Rasila declared and extended a shadow blade. "Where is the enemy?" She looked around, eagerness in her eyes. "I presume foes who would set a bomb off in the center of a city street deserve not even your generous mercy?"

While most of the other motorists had fled the area, a few hid in nearby alleys or close to the front of buildings, their phones out to film everything.

"Do what you need to," Alison replied. "And, yeah, I'm not in a generous mood." She raised her hands and prepared to destroy the slabs that penned the car in. Before she could cast her spell, the side slab cracked and collapsed into a pile of stones to reveal the car. Vincent stepped out, his wand in hand and a deep scowl on his face.

"Talk about fucking overkill." He growled his disgust,

then looked at the gathered Drow. "Huh? Who the hell are they?"

Miar sneered at him. "Is this one responsible for the bomb? He has the look of a coward."

He lowered his wand and frowned at Alison.

"They helped save your life, Vincent." She extended her own shadow blade. "And you're right, Rasila, this isn't over." She nodded at the two princesses. "There are two wizard assassins. Ruthless killers who think nothing of killing innocents as you saw for yourself."

"It's always enjoyable to kill enemies without political considerations," Rasila replied. "I would hope they might be worthy foes, but considering their plan, I doubt it."

Miar glowered. "I understand. For now, your enemies are our enemies."

Vincent's guards exchanged glances and sprinted away, terror on their faces.

"You bastards," he screamed. "You'd better get the hell out of Seattle."

"Everyone around the coward, the assassins are here for him," Alison shouted and rushed toward Vincent.

"Oh, come on, Dark Princess," he groaned. "That's not fair."

The Drow princesses and their retinue joined her. Drysi holstered her wand and drew two explosives knives. Mason scanned the area, his wand ready.

"Nine and twelve o'clock high," Tahir reported. "I'm getting odd thermal readings there."

Alison flung a shadow crescent in one direction. Drysi threw a dagger in the opposite direction, and Mason launched a fireball. The Drow took the hint and broke into two groups, each of which included a Drow princess.

Trained warriors with trained warrior instincts.

Her shadow crescent struck something, and a man in dark clothing appeared. A glowing shield surrounded him and his wand was in his hand. He pointed it at Alison, but a combined volley of shadow crescents from Alison, Rasila, and two other Drow carved through his shields and sliced him in half. He didn't even have time to scream.

The explosive dagger and fireball combination revealed the other hitman and depleted his shield to a thin, barely perceptible layer. He had barely begun to fall before the narrow, dark beam from the tip of Miar's sword, Drysi's other dagger, and a bright bolt of light magic from Mason's wand struck him. When the explosion and light cleared, a charred, smoking corpse with a hole through the chest lay motionless.

Alison edged away from the semi-circle around Vincent, her blade up. "Before, you told me they worked alone. Are you sure?"

He took a deep breath. His face was pale and sweat dotted his brow. "Yes, they took special pride in it."

"Tahir, do you see anything dangerous?"

"Incoming AET dropship and air ambulances about three minutes," he reported. "But every other person lingering in the area seems to be someone trying for their own viral video."

"I don't think we need the ambulances." She exhaled a sigh of relief and looked around. A smoking crater dominated the center of the street, but there been no major structural damage to the buildings and there were no wounded other than the now-deceased hitmen. She turned toward the other two princesses. "Thanks for your help. I...just thanks. I know protecting Seattle isn't probably high on your list of priorities."

Rasila released her blade. "Perhaps."

Miar nodded and sheathed her blade in one smooth motion. "I would have wished for stronger foes, but this was worth doing."

Alison nodded. "You'd better get out of here unless you want to spend the next couple of hours talking to the cops and PDA. We can talk tomorrow morning. I still have a few things to clear up."

"Until then, Princess of the Shadow Forged." Miar bowed her head. She held her hand up and a swirling portal appeared. "You have good instincts, and I see now that Rasila did not exaggerate about many things." She stepped through the portal, followed by all the other Drow with the exception of Rasila.

The Drow princess grinned. "I would tell you to learn to conceal your emotions better, Alison, but if you hadn't on the call, we wouldn't have come and you would have likely died in that explosion." Her smile faded. "Be better in the future. Do not give your life for something so banal, Alison. You're meant for more than hunting assassins." She opened a portal and retreated through it, shaking her head.

Vincent wiped the sweat off his forehead. "I guess I owe you, Dark Princess." He glanced at where the portals had been. "Or, if I understand it correctly, I guess I owe three Dark Princesses."

CHAPTER FOURTEEN

Alison almost chuckled when she saw Miar's human disguise. The muscular, armored warrior had been replaced by a pale, frail, elderly woman with stringy white hair in a loose dress. The choice stood in contrast to Rasila's consistent use of a young, attractive, and fashionable human form, complete with an added mole on her cheek for distinction.

I've let Rasila's vanity warp my perception of things. Then again, she understands that part of surviving on Earth is manipulating people's perceptions. The ultimate human dream—the ability to change your appearance on a whim.

She sat with the disguised princesses in a corner booth of a steakhouse near downtown. Rasila had contacted her as Ruby and requested her to meet there for a lunchtime meal with their mutual "new friend." Now, they sipped on water and none of the three touched their salads while they awaited their meal, which Rasila had taken the liberty of ordering before Alison's arrival. The Princess of the

Endless Shadow had also taken it upon herself to secure the booth against eavesdropping.

"Thank you both again," Alison said with a smile. "Many people could have been injured or killed. I like to think I could have contained the explosion myself, but I doubt it."

"Knowing your limits is never something to be ashamed of, Alison," Miar replied. She frowned at the plate of salad as if its mere existence insulted her. "I was more than happy to help stop the attack of two cowardly assassins."

"No, Miar, you're letting her not consider the idiocy of her actions." Rasila wrinkled her nose. "Dying for humans." She shook her head. "I understand your interest in your security business, but you shouldn't throw your life away so easily."

Alison frowned. "Even if I wasn't half-human, I won't run and let innocent people die simply to save myself."

Miar nodded. "There's no honor in letting others die when you could have prevented it."

"Believe as you want." Rasila sounded unconcerned by their opinion.

She looked at her two full-blooded Drow companions. "What exactly is the deal here? I was under the impression before that you two are kind of...well, not enemies, but you're not friends. Aren't you both interested in being queen?"

Rasila smiled. "I've made it clear I would prefer to not be your enemy, and I thought that Miar, being closer to your mindset, might potentially be interested in some kind of alliance. A little diplomacy isn't a bad thing. It's a useful skill for any future queen to have."

Alison frowned. "You decided all that without telling me ahead of time?"

"Surprise encounters are often more revealing as to the practical reality of certain things."

Miar snorted quietly. "To be honest, Alison, although I respect your bravery and strength and I wanted to meet you, this meeting means nothing otherwise. I don't support Rasila for queen, and I don't support you either. I don't question your honor, but you're not fully Drow and it would be inappropriate to lead our people."

She shrugged. "I can't say I disagree. I've told Rasila that."

"Yes, you have." The woman scoffed. "But even if you don't want to be queen, you'll still need to lend your voice to and support another. I still hope to persuade both of you to support me, but I understand that will require additional efforts on my part."

"I'm not completely persuaded that the Guardians should be removed," Miar said with a frown.

Rasila shook her head, her face a mask of disgust. "You've expressed this in the past and I have trouble believing it. You, out of all of us, are the most obsessed with tradition. The Guardians are standing in open defiance of that."

"A necessary defiance." She pointed a bony finger at Rasila and then herself. "We let Laena lead our people down a road of decadence and self-destruction. If it wasn't James Brownstone who killed her, it would have been someone else. The Fixer. King Oriceran. Any manner of being she had wronged. Now, we who were too cowardly and weak to go against her must bear the stain on our honor for failing to stop her and so forced an outsider to do it for us. Laena corrupted the Drow, and we need to find the best way to lead our people out of that corruption."

"The Guardians won't last. They don't have the personal strength or the backing of tradition." Rasila looked at Alison. "You're so concerned with innocents being harmed. It's inevitable that the Guardians will fail and a struggle will occur. People will die unnecessarily unless we unify around a strong candidate who will not be challenged, either because of personal strength or her alliances."

"Which you believe is you?" Miar scoffed and shook her head. "You spend much of your time here on Earth, playing games in the shadows. I don't trust you to be queen, Rasila."

The other Drow princess smirked. "I represent the future, Miar. The gates have begun opening. Earth and Oriceran will be entwined for much longer than either of us will live. You're too backward-thinking to become queen, but many respect you. If you back me, they will fall in line. In addition, Novati would give up and I'm already able to counter Drae's games. She'll give up for certain if all the other princesses support me." She turned to Alison. "What if Miar backed me? Would you consider it then?"

She shook her head. "I need to stay neutral."

Miar frowned. "I have not said I would back you, Rasila. You shouldn't be so presumptuous."

Alison opened her mouth to comment but stopped as

the waitress arrived with their steaks. The three Drow princesses spent the next few minutes in a tense silence while the quality of the steak pushed back a little against the unpleasant atmosphere.

"I stand by everything I've said," she said after she'd swallowed a mouthful. "I won't support anyone."

"Then you support the Guardians by default," Rasila muttered. "And Miar's at least providing them some indirect support, which means you two are forming a Guardian faction."

"I'm not in any faction," she complained. "I'm neutral."

The princess sneered. "Neutrality's a convenient fiction. All choices have implications, and you can't pretend those implications don't exist simply because they inconvenience you."

Miar narrowed her eyes. "If she doesn't support you, then you haven't proven worthy of support."

Rasila's nostrils flared. She squared her shoulders, and judging by the way she gripped her knife, Alison was half-convinced she would stab it into the other woman's throat. The tension slowly ebbed from her face to be replaced by a half-smirk. "I can't claim you don't speak the truth." She glanced at Alison. "What about Myna?"

"Huh?" She blinked. "What about her?"

Miar stiffened.

"She wanted you to become queen, didn't she?" She shrugged. "Do you think so little of her opinion? If you're not willing to support one of us, then at least you should try yourself. Otherwise, you insult her memory."

Miar frowned. "That's unfair and manipulative."

"Is it untrue?"

Alison's jaw tightened. She set her utensils down and looked at her companions. "And there's no way I can renounce my title? I've been told no before, but if I contribute to Drow instability, I should at least consider it."

Rasila laughed. "How ridiculous. Your mother ran, too. What good did it do her? Perhaps if she hadn't been weak and ran, she wouldn't have ended up the situation she did."

She bolted from her seat. "Shut the hell up," she snarled. "You don't know the first thing about my mother. She wasn't weak. Even after they tortured her for weeks, she fought her way out and killed dozens of the bastards. And as she lay dying, she didn't use the wish to save herself. She used it because she cared about someone other than herself."

Several other diners looked at her with frowns and probably wondered why they couldn't hear the heated conversation.

Alison lowered herself into her seat, her hands clenched into fists. "You don't know anything."

"I know she trusted a human, and that human betrayed her." Rasila shook her head. "Don't you understand? You don't belong here with them. Yes, you must spend some time with them, but they aren't your people like we are."

Miar glared at Rasila. "You walk a thin line."

"She needs to understand her situation." The Drow threw her hands up. "No, Alison, you can't run from what you are. It's not mere politics. You are the Princess of the Shadow Forged, and your daughters or your female descendants will be one in the future. Even if you don't like it and don't care, it doesn't matter."

She took a few deep breaths. "It changes nothing, and

don't you dare bring up my mother or Myna again like that. If you don't want to be my enemy, you will not misuse the memories of those I loved."

Rasila averted her eyes. "I admit I might have said too much."

Alison sighed and looked down. "Don't you understand my position? You say I don't belong on Earth, but I've been to Oriceran. I know I don't belong there. Yes, I had great respect for Myna's opinion. She saved me in more ways than one and she wanted me to be queen, but I also need to make sure I don't make a situation worse by bumbling into it. I'm a baby compared to you two, and despite my raw strength, I don't even have full control of my abilities. In a culture of might makes right, I'm sure that would cause trouble even when I can kick an ass or two."

Miar frowned. "Neither Rasila nor me would have been able to contain that explosion by ourselves. There's no shame in that."

"I'm not talking about things like that." She shrugged. "I know I don't have the inherent shape-shifting of Drow, but there are certain types of magics I still can't accomplish well, if at all. Myna was helping me with some of those, like improving my shadow compression for portals and shadow healing. Don't you see? I'm not strong enough to be your queen. I don't want to be your queen, and I think like a human, not a Drow."

Miar nodded slowly. "I knew Myna before she was exiled. I was very young at the time, but she was everything I aspired to be. I feel shame to this day that I didn't speak out more during her exile."

Rasila stared at Alison and obvious calculation played

125

across her face. A thin smile settled into place. "You would benefit in your security work from some of the magic you mentioned, yes?"

She shrugged. "Of course I would. What about it?"

"I can't do anything about you feeling closer to the humans, but I could help train you." She nodded at Miar. "And what of you?"

"If Myna supported you, then you have potential." Miar cut off another piece of steak. "This doesn't mean I'll support you for queen, but I think a Drow princess—even as a representative on Earth—needs to be as powerful as possible. I'd be willing to spend some time helping train you."

"I suspect we might even be able to help you more than Myna," Rasila added.

Alison gave her a confused look. "What makes you think that? I know she wasn't a royal, but she was ancient and powerful."

"And she also avoided Earth and cared little about non-shadow magic. I might not have non-shadow magic, but I'm at least aware of it." Rasila shrugged. "I've learned to be adaptable, and I suspect even Miar is a little more flexible. We might have insight that Myna lacked due to her particular circumstances."

She nodded slowly. It wasn't a terrible idea and if they both trained her, given their different political positions, it wouldn't suggest she was implicitly supporting either's claim to the throne. On the other hand, the more she involved herself with the Drow, even on a casual basis, the more enmeshed she would become in their politics.

Is it unavoidable no matter what I do? Some kind of sick destiny?

Alison sighed. "I'm having a hard time thinking of a reason why learning to use my powers more effectively would be a bad thing."

"Excellent," Rasila declared. She rubbed her hands together, glee in her eyes. "I'll be in touch."

Miar nodded. "As will I."

Should I ask them to help me with the Tapestry? No. It's not a Drow problem, and the help today was one thing. But training is different than asking them to fight and maybe kill for me.

"Thank you." She smiled. "I know you have your own reasons for doing it, but still, thank you."

CHAPTER FIFTEEN

Alison tugged at the hem of the black dress that clung to her body. The garment was bad enough, but her heels were so high, she could probably slay a dragon with them. Her hair was up in loose ringlets.

I should stop letting Hana convince me to go crazy on date night, but it's not like I could wear jeans and a T-shirt to a fancy restaurant.

Being blind for so many years destroyed any nascent concerns about clothing choices, something she repeatedly tried to explain to James when he first adopted her. Even after Shay acquired the artifact glasses to help her see in a normal manner, it was hard for her to care that much, and now that even the glasses weren't required, the habits of her earlier life remained. It wasn't that she didn't understand how to dress up, but it always struck her as vaguely pointless, if not embarrassing.

She sipped on a glass of chardonnay and tried not to let her discomfort with her appearance play out on her face. Mason had brought her to the restaurant to have a good time, and the least she could do was try to do exactly that. Her boyfriend, as usual, was stunningly handsome in his dark suit. He looked up from his halibut with a smile.

"Is this too cheesy, A?" he asked with a slight grin. "I'll admit I was surprised but happy you agreed with everything that is going on, but between Vincent, the Tapestry, Ultimate, and the Drow princess reunion, I thought we needed a normal night that didn't involve magic at all. And since it was coming up anyway…" He shrugged. "I understand if it's too cheesy."

"Happy Valentine's Day," she replied with a chuckle. "It's not cheesy. If you showed up at my office with a guitar and sang me a ballad, that would be too cheesy." She gestured to her half-eaten halibut. "And this fish is perfect. I wouldn't be surprised if they had a kitchen pixie in there using magic to make it."

Some days, I really miss the food at the School of Necessary Magic.

"You never know these days." He set his glass down. "But you're here with me now, right?"

"What do you mean? Where else would I be?"

"You looked a little distant," he said gently. "I hope you weren't worrying about a problem you can't solve tonight. It doesn't do me any good to drag you out to eat if you spend all the time worrying about something other than how dashing I look."

"No, it's just…" Her cheeks burned. "It has nothing to do with anything like that." She leaned forward. "It's kind of the opposite."

"The opposite?" Mason raised an eyebrow.

"Yeah. The dress isn't too much, is it? I don't have the curves Hana does to really pull it off, but..."

Mason grinned. "No, it's not too much. It's great. I'm your boyfriend. Do you really think I'd be upset about you wearing a sexy dress? I know you like to keep it casual but showing off every now and again doesn't hurt. And in case I've not said it enough..." He leaned closer. "I like your body a lot," he whispered.

She leaned back and her gaze darted around. "But now that you mention it, I do wonder if this is okay."

"I shouldn't have even asked." He laughed. "Oh, A, don't do this to yourself. We don't have a decent lead on the Tapestry right now, and you've said it yourself, the FBI and PDA are involved as well. It's not a Brownstone show. I think you forget sometimes that we're a security company, not the police."

"I know." Alison took another sip of her wine. "But since I saw that True Core, I know they're still in town, which means they'll try again. It's inevitable."

"It's two steps forward, one step back with you." He stroked the top of her hand. "Look, if it's not the Tapestry, then it's dark wizards. If it's not dark wizards, then it's evil technomagic billionaires, and if it's not them, then it's the Eastern Union."

She pulled her hand away. "I've chosen a life where I challenge bad people. I won't apologize for that."

"And I'm not asking you to." Mason shrugged. "I'm simply trying to remind you that it'll always be dangerous for us in one way or another, and that doesn't mean we have to stop living our lives. We have to take happiness where we can find it and deliver beat-downs when we need to. That's what I think. You're not some nun who has taken a vow to devote all her life only to fighting evil."

Alison laughed. "I'm sure my dad would have loved it if I had. Who knows? The Catholic Church might actually have that kind of thing these days."

He chuckled. "Maybe. The other thing I want you to keep in mind is that just because you're a magical security contractor, you don't have the market cornered on danger. If anything, it might be *safer* for you in a way."

"You think I lead a safe lifestyle? You constantly complain about me putting myself in danger."

"I didn't say you led a safe lifestyle." He gestured to a man across the room whose back was turned. "I meant it might be safer in relative terms."

"Safer than a guy eating at a seafood restaurant?" she asked, now more confused than ever. "I think I can safely say my job's a little more dangerous than that. Unless you're saying he's allergic."

Mason shook his head. "I'm simply picking a random man. For all I know, he's special forces who specialized in fighting rogue magical animals in some strange jungle somewhere. My point is that there are many people out there who are at risk in their jobs. Police officers, firefighters and soldiers are obvious ones, but also jobs you wouldn't think about like deep-sea fishermen, construction workers or even doctors who risk getting infected by patients."

"Okay, I follow you now. What about them all?"

"Most people on Earth aren't magicals." He shrugged. "Even AET are men and women using artifacts and technology, and they at least have a chance if something crazy happens. The average street cop might run into a rogue magical and not know what to do or a firefighter might rush into a building that some kind of summoned flame is destroying. Even before the gates started opening, people were at risk, and people always have been. You merely have to grab onto every minute of life and live it for what it is."

She laughed. "There's nothing more romantic than talking about the dangers of jobs."

"I'm only trying to keep you from falling back into old habits." He shook his finger warningly. "I think it's easy for you to obsess over an enemy and let it take control of everything in your life. This is partially my fault."

"Your fault? How?"

"I want to give you your space, and so you start to slide into forgetting to live the rest of your life—at least the part that doesn't include me. Hana would simply drag your nice butt out to a club and force you to enjoy yourself. Life doesn't begin and end with the job, A. I love you, but we also spend all day together, and I think that means I'm not always as sensitive to what you need. I think it's important for you to spend time with your friends and not worry about anything. Me, the job, your mom, anything. Just have fun, too."

Alison picked her glass up to take a sip as she considered his words. "I'll try to relax more."

"Good." Mason smiled. He picked his fork up to eat his halibut. "I'm not trying to criticize. I only want the woman I love to be happy. You deserve to be. You've already given so much to so many people. You used a wish, for crying out loud, because you were concerned that people you didn't even know would be hurt. If you quit this job tomorrow and took up singing, no one could criticize you."

"I don't want to quit."

"I know, A. You feel you have a responsibility, and I respect that. I'm not telling you to quit, and it's not exactly like I spent my life working in a library. I simply think..." A wistful smile appeared on his face. "I think more about the future lately—you and me."

Alison looked away, her cheeks burning. "I know you do, and I also know you've been patient with me even when I get too far lost in my head."

"I've told you before that you're worth waiting for. You're a very special woman in more ways than one, and I'll continue to wait for you, but that doesn't mean I can't plan now, does it? Eventually, the wait will be over."

She finished her wine and set the empty glass on the table. "No, I suppose it doesn't hurt to plan."

"Let me ask you one thing, A. *When* we get married, would you actually be willing to go on a honeymoon? A long one? I'm talking about an old-school deal where neither of us has responsibilities. The company can run itself. Ava can steer reasonable jobs to Drysi and Hana. Between them, Tahir, and Sonya, it'd be fine." Mason leaned forward, his eyes searching. "I want to spend some quality time with you without anything interfering."

"On our honeymoon?"

Wait. Did he say when and not if?

"Yes." He frowned slightly and straightened. "When that time comes. Like I said, I'm planning for the future."

"I suppose no one could complain if I took time off for

my honeymoon," she mused, her heart racing. "It's traditional."

"Yes, it is traditional." His amusement faded to be replaced by an intense stare.

Is he going to ask me here and now? Am I ready to answer? Woah.

"I...well, yes." She shrugged, her entire body burning now, and her heart threatened to escape her body. "By the time something like that happens, we'll probably be long done with the Tapestry. The Seventh Order's gone. I don't see any reason why we couldn't share a long time together." Her breathing turned ragged and shallow.

Mason's mouth quirked into a smile. "Good to know."

"It is?"

"For the future?" He picked the bottle of chardonnay up and filled her glass. "Shall we toast to the future?"

She picked her glass up. "To the future."

He clinked his against hers. "To the future."

Alison gulped the wine this time and hoped a stronger buzz would quench some of her disappointment.

Apparently, I am not only ready and willing. I'm eager. Everything will change then, exactly like it did for Mom and Dad.

CHAPTER SIXTEEN

Thoughts of romance, weddings, and Valentine's Day remained distant in Alison's thoughts the next morning. She'd gone out of her way to focus on something else as she didn't want to replace one form of obsession with another. As such, she took the opportunity to read through Jerry's notes in the personnel files on her tablet. It was something she had intended to do for some time, but life and deadly magicals always seemed to get in the way.

Mason acts like it's not a big deal, but this has been my life for a long time, all the way back to the Harriken and the School of Necessary Magic. Some people simply don't have good luck.

As a result of the way the business had been organized, Brownstone Security functioned in practical terms almost as two separate companies in the field in most weeks. The primary magical team mixed with the non-magicals at work but far less on actual jobs. Her attempts to trap the hitmen had been some of the few joint operations in recent months.

Jerry noted that he thought the organizational system

was more efficient given the different capabilities of the teams, but she sometimes worried that running things that way undermined her goal to promote magical and non-magical integration and hold her company up as a symbol of its success.

Alison frowned. Her father's agency, in a way, was far more effective in mixing together magicals and non-magicals and had been for years, but perhaps his unique background accounted for that reality.

A light knock came at the door.

She set her tablet down. "Come in."

The door opened, and Ava stepped inside. She closed the door behind her, her brow wrinkled with concern.

"Is something wrong?" Alison asked.

"Not in the sense you're likely thinking. I do have something I'm concerned about, but first, I would beg a favor."

"Sure. What is it?"

"Would you permit me to secure this room against outside listening, Miss Brownstone?" the woman asked. "It's not that I don't trust my fellow employees, but some things aren't meant for everyone to know as you yourself have stated on previous occasions."

She nodded. "Okay...uh, go ahead. Do you have a way to do that?"

There's no way she's secretly been a magical without me noticing, but she might have an artifact.

Her assistant raised her hand and spread her fingers. A small silver cube rested between her middle and index fingers. "Do you know what this is? I have reason to believe you do, but I thought it best to check."

"Yes, I've seen Senator Johnston use them. It's a silence cube. I forget the official name."

Ava walked over and set it on the edge of the desk before she sat and crossed her legs. "That's exactly what it is."

"But why do you have something like that?" she asked. "I don't sense any magic off it, so it's not a technomagic device, and from what I've seen, that kind of gadget is very rare and specialized."

"That's a good question. Although I don't intend to answer it at all, it leads into why I'm here to talk to you." The woman frowned for a moment but smoothed her expression a few seconds later. "There are additional resources available to deal with the Tapestry if they are indeed non-Oriceran extraterrestrials, and I wanted to make that very clear."

Do I push or not? I've let certain things slide.

Alison's frowned deepened. "Before we continue, I have one question for you, and I hate to do this, but I want to use a truth spell."

Ava nodded. "Do what you need to. Any questions you ask, I intend to answer honestly, but I'll be clear right now and state that there are some things I can't and won't tell you. I won't lie. I'll simply refuse to answer them."

"Fair enough." She summoned a truth orb. "Are you an agent of the United States government?"

"No," she declared and her accent somehow sounded even more English despite the simple word.

"Are you an agent of any Earth or Oriceran government?"

"No," she repeated.

The orb remained unchanged for both questions.

Her eyes held something Alison had never seen before —pleading.

If I ask the wrong question, I'll lose her. This woman has fought for me more than once, and she's supposed to only be my administrative assistant.

She sighed. "One last question. Would you ever knowingly undermine this company in a way that would lead to the harm of any of our employees?"

"Never," Ava uttered, the two syllables sharp and defiant.

Alison released the spell. "That's good enough for me. Just because my life's been a series of shared secrets doesn't mean that everyone has to live that way." She folded her hands in front of her. "Back to what you were saying."

"The Tapestry." Her assistant cleared her throat. "It might be that they are, in fact, non-Oriceran extraterrestrials, but given some of the details you highlighted in your initial statement and some of our subsequent discussions, they very well might not be. But if at any point we collect evidence that suggests a stronger possibility than not, we have better cards we can play than the PDA, especially since the Tapestry seems to operate mostly in the United States if they are indeed linked to Ultimate."

She narrowed her eyes. "You're talking about the CIA, aren't you?"

Is she former CIA? I didn't ask her if she used to be an agent of a country, only if she currently was, but why would the CIA hire a foreigner? Or she could have been MI6. I've thought so before. Many things would make sense then, but maybe she's trying to throw me off.

"The CIA does have unique experience and access to other resources that allow them to deal with such threats." Ava shrugged. "Even resources the PDA doesn't have access to."

"You've known about aliens this entire time, haven't you?" she asked.

The woman didn't respond and an expectant look settled on her face.

"What are you waiting for?" she asked.

"Aren't you going to use the truth spell?"

Alison shook her head. "I don't think you'll lie to me unless I ask the wrong question, and I think I have some idea what that might be."

"In that case, yes, I have known about aliens the entire time I've worked for you, and I've been aware for many years—long before you told me—that your father is a Vax and the truth about the Battle of LA. To be clear, I admire him for his efforts to defend this planet. I also have a passing familiarity with NOAT from a...previous life."

"NOAT? I don't know what that is."

"It's sometimes called the Floating City Squad. It's officially the CIA's Non-Oriceran Alien Taskforce. They have primary jurisdiction in the US government for handling such matters."

"Floating City Squad?" she asked. "What's up with that?"

Ava held a hand up. "Some things, I'm not at liberty to discuss. If you ever deal with them, you can ask them. Returning to the topic at hand, they have a few high-end contacts with the PDA, but their incredibly secret nature means there are far fewer people in the US government managing them, which gives them more operational freedom than many groups in the US government or even the CIA."

"Senator Johnston is involved with them, I presume?" she asked. "Since they let him face off against the Alliance, they probably have him running things."

Maybe the government's right. If people knew how close the Earth came to being destroyed not all that long ago, things might be way different.

Her companion shook her head. "He's involved with oversight in his senatorial capacity, but, no, he doesn't run it. The path is winding but eventually leads to the White House."

Alison scoffed. "I don't trust CIA alien-hunting spooks. Those people targeted my parents with weird, weird stuff that makes magic look boring in comparison. The only reason they probably didn't harass me is because I was in a secure magic school surrounded by wards. They are ruthless and dangerous."

Ava sighed. "That wasn't NOAT. That was Fortis, and that was a long time ago. Things are completely different at the CIA for a number of reasons. Director Winters broke the back of Fortis, and your father finished them off. Things aren't like they used to be. Not even close."

"Director Winters? As in Daniel Winters?"

She nodded. "I can't claim to know him well, but I do have at least passing familiarity with him."

"He helped Dad and Mom against Fortis. Him and some elf woman."

"Daisy. That's the name she used at the time, at least. Perhaps she's changed it."

"He runs alien hunting now for the CIA?" Alison sighed.

"I don't know. He still works for the government, and the government is so afraid of aliens they don't want to admit they exist. I can understand a few secrets here and there, but I'm actually sick of them."

Ava flicked her wrist dismissively. "I'm only noting that NOAT has unique resources in terms of both personnel and technology, but—and this is the big consideration—they are given relatively free reign to deploy those resources only when applied to this particular area of concern. If we confirm that the Tapestry are under their purview, I would suggest you contact Senator Johnston and ask for NOAT assistance. The mere fact that you use that acronym will speed through a lot of the normal obfuscation, but I would wait until such time as you're convinced beyond a reasonable doubt that the Tapestry are non-Oriceran aliens."

"Why?" Alison frowned. "What's the big deal?"

"Knowledge is power, Miss Brownstone, and Senator Johnston is an ally of yours, yes, but he's also a very old man who hasn't availed himself of magical life enhancement. When he retires or passes away, you can't be certain that his replacement will be as favorably inclined toward you." She frowned. "It's pointless to distrust an entire government as that is nothing more than a collection of people, but it's not pointless to distrust or trust particular people."

"Who are you, really?" she asked. "Why did you even apply for this job? I bet you could be off saving the world with James Bond or something, but you're happy managing the boring logistics for me?"

The woman shrugged, disinterest on her face. "I'm no

one special, especially in an office with a Drow princess, a nine-tailed fox, a shape-changing pet, and a former dark wizard assassin. I'm simply a woman like many others, a woman with a past. It's not even that I'm hiding it from you per se. I merely try to provide information only when it's relevant. It makes things simpler for both of us."

"I understand. And thank you for the information and suggestion, but right now, we can't even track any Ultimate users, let alone the Tapestry. Bringing in CIA alien hunters is premature."

Ava stood and smoothed her skirt. She picked the silence cube up. "Indeed. Now, if you'll excuse me." She headed toward the door.

"Ava, wait," Alison called.

"Yes?"

"What about calling in alien hunters from other countries? Like friends you might have back home?"

Her assistant shook her head. "That would be...difficult."

"Really?" She didn't try to mask the surprise in her voice.

"There's a reason I live here now instead of England, Miss Brownstone," she said quietly, a rare hint of pain in her eyes. "Mistakes were made, and worst of all..." She scoffed.

"Worst of all what?"

"I'm not sure I even regret them." She opened the door, stepped into the hallway, and closed it quietly without another word.

Somehow, that was both very surprising and not surprising at all.

CHAPTER SEVENTEEN

Alison drummed her fingers idly on the steering wheel of her Fiat as she waited at a red light. Mason had been right. She could do little about the Tapestry or Ultimate until she had more information, so there hadn't been much to do during the last week but move on with life. She instructed Ava not to schedule any new jobs for the primary teams for at least a couple of weeks. Although no one could be sure when they would finish matters with the Tapestry, the additional immediate need to neutralize Ultimate in Seattle was enough.

Rumors continued to fill the streets about magicals using Ultimate, but no one, including Vincent, could point to any particular new incident like the attack on the Red Bears. She wasn't sure if that meant people were actually using the drug or if the brutal attack had simply raised awareness and fed into a rich soup of street stories. The underworld and the authorities had acknowledged an uptick in unexplained disappearances of low-level criminal figures that might be associated with the drug. Unfortunately, neither the bodies nor witness reports to directly link Ultimate to the missing people had emerged thus far.

It feels like we're at a tipping point. Dad proved you can stop the problem by handling it on the supply side, but even the PDA is having trouble with tracking magic.

The light changed and she accelerated gently. A few details still didn't make sense to her. The man she had fought at the Red Bears' headquarters had swallowed a True Core but was obviously not a Strand, which still left a number of unanswered questions. The strange crystals seemed to be the basis of the Tapestry's power, so it made no sense for the group to hand them to random criminals. She simply couldn't understand why they would give other people more powerful crystals.

There's something I'm missing here. Maybe it's a coincidence. These True Cores might be from some hidden mine somewhere on Oriceran I don't know about and the Tapestry has nothing to do with them.

Alison frowned and turned at an intersection. For all her frustration with guarding Vincent and the last-minute appearance of Rasila and Miar, the job had been a straight-forward security matter that involved deploying her people to keep a client alive. Investigation jobs blurred the line between security work, police work, and bounty hunting.

She sighed and rolled to a stop behind a patrol car waiting at another red light. It'd been her unlucky day. She had caught the last five red lights. If she didn't know better, she would have thought Tahir and Sonya were messing with her.

Alison narrowed her eyes as something long, dark, and

thin rocketed toward the police car. It smashed into the side of the left back window of the vehicle and shattered the glass. The force of the blow pushed the car off the road and onto the sidewalk, where it impacted into the side of a brick building. The crash only narrowly missed a wide-eyed woman on her phone.

"What the hell?"

She put the car in park, threw her door open, and hurried out. The police officer lay slumped against her steering wheel, her forehead bloodied, but she was still breathing. A twisted metal pole hung half-embedded in the wall.

Poles don't twist free and throw themselves.

Her senses on high alert, she layered a shield around herself, waved her arms, and amplified her voice with a spell. "I'm Alison Brownstone. It's not safe. Everyone, run to safety. Contact the police and tell them to send the AET."

People raced down the street in the opposite direction. Unlike the crowd had with the truck, no one stopped to video anything. She stepped closer to the police car and carved through the door with her blade to free the officer. Blood seeped from the wounded woman's head and a deep gash scored her chest. She pulled the unconscious victim away from the vehicle and leaned her against the nearby wall.

Alison placed a hand on the woman's chest and chanted a healing spell. The wounds sealed, but the cop remained unconscious.

Should I wake her?

She straightened quickly and turned when she caught

movement out of the corner of her eye. Two shirtless men jumped from the roof of a nearby building, their veins and eyes black. They lacked the claws of the man she had fought in the junkyard, but light blue scales covered their skin.

One man grinned. "Woah, Julian. Are we lucky or unlucky?"

The other man smirked. "We're lucky, Gavin."

Alison summoned a shadow blade. "Why?" she demanded.

"Why what, Brownstone?" Gavin replied. He staggered forward, his movements erratic and unsteady. "Why are you here? Why am I here? Why are any of us here?"

Julian laughed and swayed. "Good question!"

She pointed her shadow blade at Gavin. Both men stood across the street a few yards from one another. No one else remained outdoors, but a traffic drone circled overhead.

"If you wanted a piece of me, you should have simply attacked me directly," she shouted.

"Huh?" He laughed. "Isn't that exactly what we're doing?"

Alison frowned when she sensed another magic source behind the two men. A few seconds later, a short-haired woman appeared out of thin air, as dark-veined and black-eyed as the two men. The odd features contrasted with her bleached blonde hair. Her mouth twitched uncontrollably.

"I'll give you this chance, right here and now, to surrender." She made a slicing motion with her free hand. "I'm more interested in where you got the Ultimate from than in hurting you."

"The mighty Alison Brownstone," the woman intoned. "How long can you last when everyone's stronger? A day? A week? A month?" She pointed down the street at a distant fleeing man. "Run along, Brownstone. This is our town now."

Julian nodded. "Elise is right."

Alison's gaze darted at each of the three Ultimate users. None of them carried their wands.

If this new form of Ultimate does that to witches and wizards, what would it do to an elf or a gnome?

She shuddered.

We need to stop it before it spreads, but we need to know where they get it from. It must be the Tapestry, and they have to be somewhere close to the city.

"From what I've seen, this purer form of Ultimate doesn't only change your body but also your mind," she called to the trio. "I understand having enhanced power, but why do something so stupid?"

"What's stupid?" Elise countered and continued to twitch. "We'll test the Ultimate, and then..." Her head jerked a few times. "Whispers. Somebody shut the whispers up."

Gavin frowned. "It's okay, Elise. We just have to work through them."

"I can help you," Alison insisted and lowered her weapon. "There are obviously side-effects."

"Side-effects?" Julian snarled. He stepped forward, his movements unsteady. "Not side-effects. Marks of our strength. We heard all about it, Brownstone. How you were almost killed in the junkyard because of Ultimate."

She shook her head. "I don't know where you got your

information, but that's not true." She lifted her blade again. "Surrender. I can help you. Since I have no idea who you are, it means you probably aren't completely worthless. There's still a chance for you. Help me and the cops stop Ultimate."

Elise's eyes widened. "She didn't ask for Brownstone's blood, but it has to be worth something."

"Who? Blood?"

The three users all turned to grin at one another before they pivoted toward her again.

Yeah. This will end well.

Alison flung stun bolts in rapid succession at her three opponents. Elise fell back and her eyes rolled toward the back of her head, but the two men barely even flinched. Julian growled and threw his arm up. A bright fireball roared into existence and hurtled toward her. She flung herself out of the way and it exploded against the side of the police car.

I have to keep them away from the cop. Damn it.

She responded with two light bolts to the men's exposed chests. The attack forced them back a few feet and charred their skin. Unlike the man at the junkyard, their wounds glowed as they began to heal. Gavin's movement became a blur as he barreled forward. She had no time to even think but instinctively raised her shadow blade and stabbed him through his head. The man screamed and fell forward. She yanked her weapon out and let him fall heavily and he twitched on the roadside.

Julian hissed and raised his hands. Flames swirled between them and fueled a growing fireball. Alison leapt aside before the man launched his attack. The fireball exploded a couple of yards away from Gavin, blasted asphalt in a flurry of debris, and charred the wounded man.

Alison fired a shadow crescent, but it struck a shield that shimmered into existence with the strike.

"You've lost," she shouted. "Both of your friends are down. Give it up."

This guy is actually using his magic and isn't merely a feral monster. I don't know which worries me more.

The closing sirens joined the familiar roar of a dropship.

Her adversary raised his arms, and large chunks of asphalt ripped from the street around him. "Power, Brownstone. Power you can't even begin to imagine. That's what she gave us."

"Who?" Alison asked. "Elise?"

"Elise?" Julian's laugh turned plaintive. "Yes. She gave it to Elise, too." He screamed and launched the tar missiles toward her.

She grunted as the collision bowled her over. Her shields saved her from anything other than a minor sting. Several stray pieces of asphalt smashed into the wall behind her and sprayed smaller pieces to pepper the area.

Julian rushed over to a stop sign and ripped it from its moorings with ease. An obvious pulse of magic accompanied the action and a dull red light suffused the sign. Alison extended her wings and launched upward seconds before he hurled it at her. The large missile continued across the street until it struck an unfortunate ATM. A massive explosion destroyed the machine and the wall around it.

The dark form of the approaching dropship grew larger in the distance. An AET team was almost there.

Huh. They must have already been in the air. Returning from something else or merely on patrol?

Alison circled her opponent. She released her blade and pelted him with a steady stream of light bolts. The man grunted at her barrage and the shimmer of his shield weakened with each strike until her attacks plowed into his chest, arms, and legs. He fell to his knees with burns all over his body. They began to glow as the skin healed and burns disappeared.

"I won't let you win, Brownstone," the man bellowed. Streams of light arced from his body to fuel a growing ball. "If I go down, you go down."

"Crap," she muttered, conjured a new shadow blade, and dove directly toward the screaming man. She chose the only strategy she knew was foolproof and severed his head with one quick swing. His attack rocketed into the air and only narrowly missed a nearby building.

I hope I didn't help him shoot down a satellite.

Alison descended slowly and dragged in a deep breath. She released her wings and blade and glanced at the prone Elise. At least this time, there was a survivor to interrogate. A dropship with an open bay door arrived overhead. A half-dozen cops in power armor leapt from the back and fell directly toward the embattled intersection. Their thrusts packs fired at the last second, and they landed with a synchronized and resounding thud to brandish a mixture of railguns and rifles.

Even I'd have trouble if they opened up with all that hardware. They probably already have anti-magic bullets loaded, too.

She took another deep breath, her stomach tight. The first few moments of an AET encounter were always tense. She never knew how they would react.

One of the AET officers turned toward her. The opaque helmet concealed his features, and his transmitted voice sounded hollow as he said, "Witnesses reported a half-dozen men."

No orders to stand down. That was promising.

Alison shook her head. "Only the three." She gestured toward Elise. "She's the only one still alive. They mentioned that some woman gave them the Ultimate, but they didn't give a name." She pointed to the unconscious cop in the opposite direction. "I stabilized her, but you should probably have her checked out."

Elise screeched and pushed herself up. A translucent shield surrounded her. "How dare you!"

Alison directed a stun bolt at the woman, but the new shield absorbed the attack.

The AET officers all aimed their weapons.

"Stand down, or you will be fired on," bellowed a cop.

Elise's eyes slid to the side until she stared at the unconscious uniformed officer.

"Don't do it." Alison shunted magic into her legs and shook her head. "You don't have to die here."

"I was supposed to be a goddess," the woman shrieked and raised her palm.

She released the magic in her legs and flew toward the wounded officer. The deranged attacker conjured a twisted, barbed spear and launched it toward the cop as well. The projectile struck Alison instead and bounced off her shield.

The boom of railguns and crack of rifles followed. Elise danced as the AET's assault ripped through her defenses and then her body. Alison grimaced and looked away as the police finished their grim work.

I need to end Ultimate.

CHAPTER EIGHTEEN

Vincent looked at Alison from in front of her desk, an easy smile on his face like he had no cares in the world. Despite what Miar had said, the kind of man who could pull off a lavender suit and gold chains could never be called a coward.

The old Vincent is back. He doesn't have that air of fear around him.

She gestured toward her closed office door. "I was surprised when I called you that you said you wanted to meet me at my office instead of the True Portal."

"The death of those two hitmen has changed my situation, and I'm trying to explore all the aspects of that." He shrugged. "And there's a certain reality to what happened that I might as well lean into. What a man accepts is what a man can control."

"Meaning what exactly?" She frowned in confusion.

He grinned. "It's pointless to pretend I'm a disinterested third-party when the entire city knows you saved my ass from those hitmen. Some people call me Brownstone's

Bitch." He shrugged and maintained his smile. "I'll make sure the nickname goes away, but the perception won't."

Alison nodded. "And that's messed with your business?"

Vincent shook his head. "It's not hurt my business. If anything, people are more interested in talking to me because they think I might tell them something about you they don't know." He held a hand up. "Just so you know, I don't tell them anything that's not already out there, although more than a few people have talked about how you have a secret army of Drow. The cops were tightlipped about that explosion the other day, but pictures out there on the net showed you had a group of Drow with you."

"Secret army of Drow?" She scoffed. "They are more like…distant cousins who constantly stop by for unannounced visits, but yes, those Drow did help me limit that explosion." She sighed and shook her head. "But this isn't about me or the Drow. This is about Ultimate. Things are getting worse. I wasn't sure before, but there is now a clear escalation with the missing people and an attack on a cop in broad daylight. The police are talking about borrowing AET help from other cities and starting active patrols." She shrugged. "I need to know whatever you know. I can't imagine this is good for business as you would define it, and I won't allow these people to wander around town and attack people simply to prove something. Were you able to find out anything about what I asked you to look into?"

He nodded. "I've confirmed that whoever is dealing in town is a woman, but no one seems to have a detailed description and so far, all the Ultimate users have ended up dead or missing. There is no word on what organization she works for, her name, or anything like that." He snickered. "You'd think people would lose their interest given what keeps happening, but some are greedy."

"You mentioned Alphonse Tatum before," Alison commented. "Do you still think he's connected?"

"I've still heard rumors that he's in town, but I don't know if he has anything to do with this or not. No one's mentioned Tatum being the one dealing. It's all this woman." Vincent grinned. "She's apparently a looker with silver hair, but there are no other details. I know yours is more white, but maybe you started a trend."

"Funny."

"I know."

She folded her arms as she pondered the information. "I feel like I'm getting closer to an answer, but it's not enough to move on."

Tahir and Sonya's efforts on the web had proven fruitless. Whoever was dealing the Ultimate, whether they were affiliated with Tapestry or not, had a remarkably old-fashioned and analog approach to business. There were no trails for them to follow other than the occasional rumor on a message board that only reiterated what she already knew.

"I'm doing what I can." He shrugged. "You know I owe you. The whole damned city knows I owe you."

"I know. I'm simply frustrated." She pinched the bridge of her nose. "I was lucky the other day. The next time an Ultimate user attacks in public, more people might die. Oh, that reminds me—have you heard anything about the blood? I don't know if they were only being weird when they mentioned it, but I suspect not."

He nodded. "That checks out, too. People are saying

that the woman doesn't want money for Ultimate but the blood of magicals."

Alison grimaced. "I'll have to pass that on to the cops. That might explain some of our missing persons."

"Yes. There's a lot you can do with blood. I've never been into that kind of magic, but I asked around among a few contacts who are, and they don't know anything about it. Whoever is doing it isn't part of their normal scene, and they're kind of pissed."

"Why?"

"Because it's already hard doing blood magic without people being suspicious of you, even criminals." He uttered a dark chuckle. "It's freaky and people don't trust you, and now, they have to worry about people thinking they're the ones messing things up in town."

"Messing things up?" she asked. "The underworld is that upset about Ultimate?"

Vincent didn't respond right away. His smile faded. "Everyone has their own agenda, Dark Princess, but most people are like me. They understand a certain balance is necessary to run a profitable business, legal or otherwise. I don't think anyone minded the idea of Ultimate here, but it's not played out like it did in the few other places it's popped up."

"Oh?"

Vincent tucked his hands under his armpits and frowned. "In those places, the Ultimate was different and not only because of the wand stuff. If everything I've heard and you heard was right, it's because it wasn't as pure. A few guys here and there took the drug and received more power, but they weren't totally whacked out. It ended up being nothing more impressive than the equivalent of buying a bigger gun. The feds, cops, and your dad cleaned it out without too much trouble.

"And the guys doing Ultimate were smart about it. They didn't think it made them gods. They didn't go out and pick fights on the street. Here, they're being stupid and causing trouble." He shook his head. "More AET, more PDA, more cops, and more bounty hunters. People know what to expect from you, but they don't know what to expect from everyone else." He grunted with disgust. "Seattle's already a hard place to make a living, and we don't need outsiders making it harder. Right now, you're not the only one interested in finding out who is selling the Ultimate. Half the gangs in the city have bounties on it." His grin returned. "I'm making a little cash cross-selling the info. I assume you won't mind if some Eastern Union or Triad asshole ends the Ultimate problem for you."

Alison frowned. "I'd prefer there not be a gang war."

"This isn't about territory. I've even heard some of the groups are sharing intel." He laughed. "Think about that. All these dangerous criminals are getting together and acting like the cops to find and eliminate a drug dealer. They get it, just like you get it. The longer this Ultimate situation continues, the worse things will get. After all, before the Red Bears, it was the Eastern Union who was attacked. People don't respect territories or gangs, and everyone here is convinced that whoever is behind it doesn't care about taking over Seattle, and that's the real insult."

"Why is that? Wouldn't that make them less of a worry?"

"No, because it means they don't care at all about what mess they leave behind." His smile reappeared. "And most of them are looking for you to fix it, even though they're keeping an ear and eye out."

She rolled their eyes. "I'll stop Ultimate, but not because all the gangsters are afraid."

"Sure." Vincent looked around her office. His smile remained strong, but a hint of concern had slid into his eyes. "I don't have much more than that about Ultimate, but I did hear something that might worry you."

"Worse news than a dangerous new form of a drug flooding Seattle and driving magicals nuts?" she asked. "The only thing I can say is at least it doesn't involve dark wizards waking up ancient Oriceran weapons of mass destruction."

"I've heard rumors that the attack on the cop the other day wasn't random." He leaned forward, his expression now serious. "That the whole thing was planned."

She shrugged. "I already knew that. They admitted it."

He shook his head. "I'm saying it goes deeper than that. You see, the way the word has come out on Ultimate is that it's something that turns even a weak magical into someone strong. Really strong. That's the whole point. It can help someone who didn't have a chance become something more."

Alison nodded. "That's true. Even though I've won against the Ultimate users I've fought, it took more effort than it would normally. If it's about amplifying magic power and they were already weak, I worry about what would happen with someone who was already strong. And, from what I've seen, it frees wizards and witches from having to use a wand, which is a huge advantage in and of itself. There's no way to easily disarm them, for one thing."

"Well, yeah, but the thing is, Dark Princess, if someone wants to prove they're strong, they have to defeat someone who is known to be strong. Exactly like in prison—go up to the biggest guy and punch him on the first day." He gestured toward her. "That means more people will come knocking on your door because you're the Dark Princess. Unless you get your dad to move here, I think you're in for more trouble."

"There's nothing I can do about people wanting to fight me." Alison frowned. "I'll stick close to Brownstone Security and my house for a while, I guess. I don't want anyone else to be caught up in an attack. That cop could have been killed, and I can only imagine what would happen if someone attacks me at a coffee shop or restaurant."

"Yeah. By the way, it's funny you mention people being weak." Vincent scratched his eyebrow. "That's the other thing I've heard. It's like whoever is dealing Ultimate is deliberately not seeking out more powerful people as customers. It's all witches and wizards with fairly weak skills and power. Not a single Oriceran either."

"That's not crazy. It might only work on a certain type of magical. Like a certain biology, for example, and the Oricerans might not be interested." She shrugged. "And the dealers might not want too much competition from someone by making them too powerful. Given all the strange side-effects, someone who is already strong might not feel the need." She sighed. "This was so much easier for my dad in Vegas."

He chuckled. "A little family competition, huh?"

She shook her head. "This is my city, and I don't want people hurt in my city."

"I understand. If I knew the address of the bitch selling it, I'd give it to you right away."

"And what about the other thing I asked you about yesterday?"

"Those Tapestry guys you mentioned? No one's heard about anyone like that on the streets. Whoever the woman selling the Ultimate is, she doesn't call herself Tapestry."

With the PDA now actively and openly investigating the Tapestry, there was little reason for her to keep them a secret from others. She doubted Vincent would stumble upon anything about them being alien, and despite Ava's suggestions, she grew doubtful with each passing day that the Tapestry were anything more than strange wizards who had let their magic warp their minds.

Alison nodded. "Just keep an ear out. I have my reasons for believing they might be involved."

"Sure thing." He stood and straightened his lapels. "As always, Dark Princess, it's a pleasure doing business with you, but next time, I think we'll do this at the True Portal again."

"Why is that?"

He grinned. "You don't have any martinis."

CHAPTER NINETEEN

Alphonse paced the hotel room, a deep scowl on his face. "Worthless fools. All of them. I give them power, and they squander it because their spirits are weak and their minds soft. They don't deserve what I've given them." His hand clenched into a fist. "They'll ruin everything I've worked for, all my careful plans and research."

Mirela watched from the couch, her own expression a studied calm. "We expected a certain amount of this kind of thing. These are hardly your first losses. Don't worry, Alphonse. You can recover from this. None of the men or women lost are worth consideration, and most who have been lost were not stable enough for further research anyway."

"You're a good and loyal servant, Mirela, but you fail to see the big picture." He stopped and spun toward her. "There needs to be a balance of factors. That's the problem." He shook his head. "The experiments need field testing for proper adjustment but now, these idiots go directly to Brownstone rather than limit themselves to more reasonable targets. They were supposed to restrain themselves and mainly target other vermin." He frowned. "I've already gone through most of the last batch of Cores. There are so few who are compatible, and the Tapestry refuses to give me any samples from their own men for calibration." He sneered. "Yet they approached me about the experiments, to begin with, because of their lack of creativity."

"You'll find the solution, Alphonse," she insisted. "You always do. This is merely a temporary setback. As long as you gain some data from each experiment, you'll achieve success."

He closed his eyes and took a deep breath. When he opened them, his calm expression had returned and he nodded. "You're right. I'm letting my emotions get the best of me, but that doesn't change the fact that Seattle has become a difficult environment to operate in, even though it is, by far, the prime environment for my experiments."

"Is it really that difficult? I've had no trouble evading the authorities."

"The PDA, FBI, and police have all intensified their efforts, let alone the criminals and Brownstone. Perhaps we pushed too hard with our demands that they bring the blood and raised too much attention, but it was the quickest way to gather what we needed and redirect suspicion. This isn't like Dallas, Las Vegas, or any of the other test cities. This is the true chance at enhancement. We're close. I thought abandoning a certain level of caution wouldn't jeopardize the project, but I failed to properly account for the black hole that is Alison Brownstone."

Mirela nodded. "Do you plan to leave Seattle, then?"

Alphonse shook his head. "There's something about the background magical environment that alters the process in subtle ways that even I barely understand. I suspect it has something to do with the destroyed kemana, but I'm dubious that I could achieve these kinds of results in another city." He nodded at her. "You're one of the few truly stable enhancements I have achieved. Even if you're not from this city, the process was achieved here. Besides, the Tapestry aren't likely to give me other Cores for anywhere other than Seattle. They've made that clear. Their attention is more focused here now for whatever reason."

"Perhaps you could simply wait and give the situation time to calm. It's not impossible."

"It would be too much of a risk to the momentum of the project," he countered. "No, it's been difficult to keep the Tapestry engaged as long as I have, and I suspect that any departure from my immediate plans will be treated as a failure. I still need them. I'll remain in Seattle to finish the plan. First, I will isolate the exact method to produce a stable enhancement. Second, I will complete my research into how to produce a True Core from a living subject. If we can propagate the True Core, we'll have no use for the Tapestry at all."

"Then what do we do for now?" She rested her gloved hands in her lap. "Tell me what you need me to do to help you succeed, Alphonse. Anything you need."

He walked over to the window to stare out at the bay, his hands folded back his back. "We will approach this intelligently. The authorities are a mere inconvenience. They've done a very feeble job of tracking or stopping my efforts before. I've let them have a few victories to convince themselves they've achieved something. No. They aren't the true threat."

"And James Brownstone?" Mirela asked. "What of him? Does he represent a threat?"

Alphonse scoffed. "That barbecue-addled thug stopped nothing but a middleman. I'll admit that I had further plans for Las Vegas that he disrupted, but such is the path of all progress. Seattle is proving a far better testbed for my research than either Las Vegas or Los Angeles. Although his example is proof of my concern. Unlike in Vegas, a disruption to the Seattle experiments would be devastating, and yet again, a Brownstone is involved. There's only one practical solution left to enable me to stay here and continue until I have the results I need. I need a least a few more months, but I doubt I'll have them, at this rate. I begin to want to curse the Brownstone name."

"You need to kill Alison Brownstone," she declared. She understood why they had avoided it earlier, especially with the difficulties of achieving a stable enhancement, but more recent successes offered hope, including some of her own changes.

Alphonse smiled. "Exactly. She's strong but not invulnerable. I would rather not engage her at all, but now that she's become a focus in Seattle, we have no choice. Once she's dead, we'll have a window in which to complete the experiments before a new equilibrium is reached, and then, we can abandon this city. If I've achieved my goal, I'm confident the Tapestry will continue to supply me for some time and we can dispense with them when it better suits our needs."

"And what if her father comes after that? Won't it create the same problems?"

He shook his head. "There'll be little he can do. If his daughter can't find us, there's no reason to suspect he can, and no one will be foolish enough to face him. The problem is that she's too easy to find and keeps attracting my experiments, let alone potential servants." He turned away from the window. "But I want to be careful about this. Wasting resources on an assassination is pointless unless you can be assured of success. Baiting her will be easy enough." He stared at the ground. "She's powerful on her own and not impossible to defeat, but with so many strong allies, gathering the necessary forces might be difficult in the time we have. We will need to separate her from her allies."

Mirela's breath hitched. It was her chance to prove herself to Alphonse. He had given her so much and uplifted her from a position where she was nothing. Her family of dark wizards considered her a sad blot on their line because her magical ability had been almost non-existent. They cast her out when they had grown weary of her, but they'd wasted the years and not prepared her for any other existence than to simply circulate among the elite dark families. A witch with no real magic and a dark family upbringing was one who would inevitably suffer—and she had, in so many ways.

But he had seen through all that to the potential locked inside her. He had looked at her soul and understood that she deserved as much power as her family enjoyed. They had been born into it without true work, but she had suffered for it. She had earned it.

In the end, despite all their lofty rhetoric, the dark wizards proved to be nothing more than elitists who sought to control others, but Alphonse would do the opposite. He would grant power to the worthy rather than claim that power made one worthy and would promote a true meritocracy. But he needed help. His dream couldn't be achieved alone. The faithful would be rewarded.

"I have an idea…" she began and smiled softly. "Allow me, Alphonse, to lead this effort. I'm confident that with my plan, I can handle Alison Brownstone."

He looked up and nodded slowly. "Then do so for the good of my cause, Mirela. Destroy Alison Brownstone."

The Overseer stood near the door to the featureless circular white room and surveyed the suited, nondescript, brown-haired Weavers who lined the walls. Everything was suboptimal. Too many pieces were subdivided, and the plan needed to be accelerated or they risked failure. Certain actions had been taken based on certain calculations, and anomalies now interfered with the Tapestry's ability to accurately determine the next course of action.

"The Seattle situation is reaching a critical point," he began. "Analysis indicates over a seventy-four percent possibility that Alison Brownstone has already discerned the link between the Tapestry and Ultimate. This increases the risk of a direct attack on our forces and a further disruption of the plan. The recovery of the target has become paramount."

One of the Weavers tilted his head. "What of the

promises to Strands of increased power? What of the experiments? All difficulties can be ameliorated with the application of enough resources."

"Tatum believes we're unaware that he is taking countermeasures." The Overseer raised his hand and an image of a smiling Alphonse appeared in the center of the room. "His research has proven the greater enhancement possibilities with the baseline genetic template as we suspected. However, there are no other significant increases in utility we can foresee if we continue to support him. Therefore, we will shift our focus. The research is a dead end. We need to improve adaptability and bring additional Strands over. With greater numbers of Strands and Cores, we can recover the target. Once we have that, we will be able to achieve maximum adaptability and reorder the Strands for direct control and unification."

"What should we do about Alphonse Tatum?" a Weaver asked.

"I will decide that when the time is right."

CHAPTER TWENTY

Omni lay on his back in the form of a small brown parrot and batted at Hana's finger with his feet— his attempt to wrestle. He made a soft noise, somewhere between a chirp and a squawk.

If you didn't know he could turn into a killing machine, you would think he was the cutest thing in the world, Alison thought.

"You're such a good little boy," the fox cooed. "A good little boy."

Or, in Hana's case, you don't care if he's a killing machine.

Alison stared at the strange pet. She had assumed he would be at the source of their next encounter with the Tapestry, but they had abandoned their efforts and gone underground, either out of fear or calculation. Their potential link to Ultimate suggested a more sinister agenda than she had believed before, given the rapid body count associated with the drug.

"What would you do if he wanted to leave?" she asked and nodded at Omni.

Hana continue to play with the bird and smiled at him as she spoke. "It's not like he hasn't had any opportunity. I've left the window open before when he was in forms that could have gotten him out there, and he's never interested in going anywhere without me. I only use a leash because I don't want some busybody calling animal control on me." She raised her hand, and Omni jumped back onto his feet. He flapped his wings and flew to her shoulder where he uttered a single squawk.

"I'll admit there were times I wondered if we should have handed him over," Alison murmured. "I didn't know if it was worth risking everyone over an animal, even a special animal. I worried about it a lot."

The fox frowned. "I'm only not mad about that because you didn't. Otherwise, I would have had to claw your eyes out."

She chuckled. "If there is one thing I learned from my parents, it's not to give in to people who try to intimidate you when they say they're trying to help you. No matter what they say their reasons are, they're usually the last people to trust." She frowned as she considered everything that had happened in the last couple of weeks and every decision she had made. "And that seems to be appropriate here. I don't know what the Tapestry has planned, but they've repeatedly demonstrated that they don't care about hurting people. For all we know, Omni was created to hunt them and that's why they are so interested in capturing him."

Omni fluttered over to Alison's shoulder and squawked. He reached over to pull a few strands of her hair.

"All I've ever wanted to do is protect people, both the

innocent and the people I love," she murmured. "But I have to be careful. This situation has me thinking about that all the time."

"Why is that?" Hana grinned. "You're Alison Brownstone, the Dark Princess. You're such a tough chick that Rasila thinks you have a good chance at the Drow throne. You don't have to be careful. People have to be careful of you."

"That's the problem. Escalation." Alison shrugged. "We're seeing that now. Because I'm powerful and growing more powerful, I attract the attention of powerful people, whether they are Drow, criminals, or whoever. I have to be careful to make sure I don't bring more trouble to this city than I resolve. If I do, I should simply retire on an island somewhere."

"Please." Her friend rolled her eyes. "How many times have you saved this city? How many clients have you helped, even before you owned this company?" She smiled softly. "You saved me from myself and the Eastern Union."

"I know what you're saying, and I get it. I really do. And my dad went through the same thing. Heavy is the crown and all that." She shook her head. "Sometimes, it's only a matter of going through enough guys until everyone finally gets the point, and sometimes, it makes me wonder." She reached over to scratch the back of Omni's neck. "Let's hope the Tapestry gets the point sooner rather than later."

A distant ringing jarred demandingly in Alison's ear. She groaned and blinked her eyes open to be confronted by darkness. The noise wasn't distant at all. It came from her nightstand.

Wait. Is that my...phone?

She rolled over to grab the offensive device.

"This is why you use do not disturb," Mason mumbled.

"I don't think I'll ever be able to use that. If someone calls me in the middle of the night, they probably have a good reason." She looked at the screen. "Vincent? Why the hell is he, of all people, calling me at 4:37 AM?"

"Because he's a sadistic dick?" her boyfriend responded, his face still half-covered by the pillow.

Alison connected the call. "I assume you're not simply being a sadistic dick, Vincent?"

He snickered on the other end. "I'm hurt, Dark Princess. No, I'm not trying to be a dick, let alone a sadistic one. I'm trying to make up for the fact that you saved me from being blown into dust by two crazed magical hitmen. I'm sure I'll come to my senses soon enough and remember to charge you far more than I have been since then, so keep that in mind."

She sat and rubbed her eyes. "The sun's not even up yet. Don't scumbags know you can't cause trouble before the sun's up?"

"Well, I always assumed that was how it worked. All the worst things happen in the day. It's why I prefer nighttime. Plenty of places to hide, but fewer people going around to annoy you."

"Sure, sure." She yawned. "So, what's this about? I assume it's important?"

"I think so, but I'll leave that to you to decide." Vincent sighed. "I had a gentleman call at my place, you see. I'm not totally unaccustomed to people showing up at odd hours given the nature of my business, but in most cases, those people are closer acquaintances and friends rather than people with whom I am not otherwise familiar. You know how I am. I like to hold court at the True Portal, but I couldn't turn this man away."

"Why? Did he come with a truck full of gold?" Alison scoffed.

He snickered. "Nope. it's because he was rather obviously under the influence of Ultimate, and such people are your area of extreme interest at the moment."

Her heart rate kicked up and the fatigue swept out of her mind. "Ultimate?"

Mason frowned and sat. He turned on the lamp next to the bed.

"Yes," Vincent replied. "The guy had the black veins and black eyes I've heard everyone mention, including you. He didn't seem entirely right in the head, so I decided not to give him any reason to get agitated. I still haven't replaced my bodyguards since those two bastards ran out on me, and I'm a wizard who likes subtlety more than fireballs. I'd have a hard time in a normal fight, let alone against someone on the pure form of Ultimate."

Alison took a deep breath and released it slowly. "And what did Mr. Ultimate want with you?"

"He wanted nothing from me. I'm simply the tool in this scenario. A mere conduit."

"I don't understand."

He sighed. "I told you the other day. Many people are now interested in me because they think I have special access to you. This man made it clear he was interested in you, not me."

She frowned. "He wanted information on me? It's not like my house and business locations are national secrets. Or did he hope you had secret information on me?"

"No, he didn't want information on you. He wanted information given to you directly by me. More specifically, he wants me to give you a message."

Wait. Could it be?

"I see. Okay, Vincent, I want to be very clear about something. Are you safe right now? If you aren't, I will come right away. I didn't go through all that trouble to save your ass so some cranked-up reject wizard could murder you to send a message to me."

He laughed. "Ah, I'm touched, but no, I'm fine. And that's not the kind of message he planned to send, but you'll be disturbed anyway. He asked me to deliver the message, and he asked me what it would cost. I told him I'd do it for free, and he seemed satisfied. He wandered off, and I called you a couple of minutes later once I made sure he wasn't coming back to rip my head off."

"Okay," she replied. "What's the message?"

The information broker clucked his tongue. "He was a little incoherent at times, so I'll summarize. Basically, he wanted you to know that the people behind Ultimate are angry with you because you keep killing the users and otherwise messing things up for them."

Alison rolled her eyes. "And they think that'll stop me?"

"Well, from what he attempted to say, the gist was that they're challenging you. He gave me an address. Basically, he said you need to come to that address as soon as possible to face them, or they'll send guys on Ultimate into several public locations and they'll start killing people." Vincent delivered the chilling message with the casual tone of a man who described next week's restaurant plans. "They said you need to come to them alone because if the police arrive instead of you, they'll carry out the plan. They also said if any of your people accompany you, they'll carry out the plan."

She swallowed. "I see. And did they give a deadline?"

"No. The guy said, and I quote, 'Lots of people are out during lunchtime. It would be a shame if something happened to them.' Then he started going off about whispers or something. I couldn't quite understand it."

Her jaw tightened and heat trickled into her face.

That's how they want to play it? Fine. Those bastards.

"Thank you, Vincent," she responded coldly. "Send the address as a message. I'll take it from there. If they stop by later, you can tell them I'm on the way."

"Actually, I won't see them for a while, Dark Princess." He chuckled. "There was another slight reason for the delay in calling you. I'm taking a little jaunt out of Seattle for a few days. No offense, but I don't want to risk getting killed twice so close together, and I don't trust that freak to not come back and paint that message with my blood. I'm already on my way to the airport."

"That's fine." She nodded. "By the time you come back, there will be no more Ultimate threat. Send me that address in the next minute." She ended the call.

Mason frowned. "A, what's going on?"

She summarized the situation quickly. Her phone chimed with the address halfway through her explanation.

He rolled to the side of his bed and stood. "What's the plan?"

Alison tossed her phone on the nightstand and headed toward her closet. "The plan is to go to the address and kick their asses. I can't take the chance that it might be a bluff. Too many people might die before AET or someone else shows up and stops an Ultimate rampage."

The life wizard shook his head. "This couldn't be more of a trap if they carved *'WARNING, TRAP'* into the side of Mount Rainer. I know you're tough but going into this on their terms isn't a great idea."

"Of course it's a trap." She threw her closet open and yanked a pair of jeans off a hanger. "It's a well-baited one, but I'm not a total moron, either. We won't follow all their terms. I think they're mostly interested in getting me there alone, but I intend to call the cops and the PDA. If I'm there first, whoever is responsible can try to kill me, and I'll be fine until everyone else—including you guys—sweeps in. Plus, if the city's on alert, they can stop any Ultimate users who might rear their ugly heads to cause trouble." She shimmied into her jeans. "The only thing I don't understand is why this doesn't feel like the Tapestry."

He dressed hastily in a pair of his jogging pants and a T-shirt. Not exactly the most epic of ass-kicking outfits, but who cared?

"You don't think it's them?" he asked.

She shook her head. "They knew enough last time to isolate and target us by ourselves. If they were ready for their next attempt, they wouldn't have to call me and threaten me to get me somewhere alone. There are many times throughout the day when I'm alone." She frowned.

"Maybe I've been wrong this whole time and this has nothing to do with the Tapestry, but from what I've seen with both the True Cores and the changes, the guys who use pure Ultimate end up too much like the Strands." She snatched a sports bra, shirt, socks, and a pair of boots from her closet.

"Remember the arms dealers?" he asked.

Alison nodded as she donned her bra and shirt. "You're saying the Tapestry is doing something similar?"

"Maybe. We hurt them badly. They might need new resources, money, that sort of thing. Maybe they're selling True Cores."

She pulled on her socks and started on her boots. "Vincent mentioned people paying with the blood of magicals, though, not money."

"Blood is a resource." Mason shrugged. "Especially to magicals."

"It doesn't matter." She tied her boots and stood with a frown. "Whoever this is, they have access to Ultimate. Even if they have nothing to do with the Tapestry or dealing Ultimate, eliminating them will make the city safer." She opened the door. "Let's go. We can call people on the way. Let Sonya sleep, though. She doesn't need the stress."

CHAPTER TWENTY-ONE

Do these Ultimate assholes think they can simply threaten people and get away with it? Even the dark wizards had the decency to try to hide their schemes. I don't care if it's Tapestry or freelancers. I'll end this today one way or another.

Alison marched up the street to a modest two-story home at the given address. She had already shielded herself and had her shadow blades ready. The only thing that kept her from blowing the house away with a channeled attack was her worry that it might damage any of the nearby homes.

If they're trying this kind of thing, it means they're desperate. I only need to make sure that if there are any actual Strands or Weavers there, I take one alive. Even if I can't make them talk, I bet the PDA can.

Or the CIA?

She scoffed. Life should have been simpler, even for her.

The dawning sun continued to push back the last lingering vestiges of darkness. She glanced down the road.

Hana, Mason, and Drysi waited in an SUV a couple of blocks away. Tahir had a drone circling the neighborhood, but he maintained a high altitude so as to not attract attention. They had no idea who or what they might face in the house other than a group of Ultimate-enhanced foot soldiers.

The PDA and police had deployed rapid-response teams on standby throughout the city. Given the early hour, they had encouraged her to press the attack. The longer she waited, the more people would be on the road. For now, the authorities had easy access to most parts of the city, and the greater bulk of the citizens hadn't ventured onto the roads yet.

Alison had convinced them she could handle whoever had sent the threat with her own personal team, which allowed them to concentrate additional resources on responding to potential reprisal attacks. She hadn't worn Tahir's receiver out of concern that her opponents would detect the magic and consider it a breach of their agreement. While she fully expected them to attack her, she didn't want to give them any reason to attack anyone else.

She took a deep breath as she walked up the concrete path to the porch and jogged up the steps. A mat reading *Bless This Mess* sat in front of the door. She frowned. The cutesy mat suggested someone else had lived there before the Ultimate thugs had taken it.

Should I knock? Just to be sure.

Actually, I should, but Brownstone style. If I'm wrong...well, I'm sure a big check will help soothe their feelings.

Her decision made, she backed up, channeled magic to her leg, and spun to kick the door. Splinters and metal erupted as it ripped off its hinges and hurtled inward. A masked man with a rifle grunted as the door pounded into him to knock his gun away and the man out.

Not exactly the bless this mess crowd.

Six other masked men with rifles stood in the living room. She didn't hesitate and fired a light bolt into the closest man before she raced forward. The crack of their rifles echoed in the small living room. Most of the men missed, but one bullet struck home. Her layered shields slowed the bullet but didn't stop it. She hissed as the slug ripped through her jacket and grazed her shoulder. Pain blossomed and spread down her arm.

Anti-magic bullets. Damn. Let's make this quick.

She whirled and stabbed a man through the heart, then kicked his falling body toward a second man and fired a bolt into another adversary's chest at point-blank range. He toppled with a death groan and the acrid smell of his burned flesh and clothing filled the air.

The survivors released a short volley and a bullet struck her thigh. She gritted her teeth and ignored the pain as she killed another man and eliminated the one who shot her with two rapid successive blasts. She layered an additional shield around herself before she slashed an enemy's throat and ran another through with her shadow blade.

I've not sensed any magic, and I don't see anyone who looks like they're on Ultimate—or even anyone who looks like a wizard.

The final surviving soldier withdrew a grenade. She launched toward him and impaled his throat before he could prime it. The device clattered harmlessly on the floor.

Alison took several deep breaths. Her thigh and shoulder throbbed. The idea of learning efficient shadow healing from Miar and Rasila grew in appeal. She'd witnessed the kind of punishment a Drow could take without having to rely on a healing potion or active spell.

This wasn't the time to lower her defenses, so she snatched a healing potion from her pocket and downed the contents. Her thigh pushed the bullet out as the wound sealed. It clinked when it landed and rolled a few inches to leave a trail of her blood.

What the hell was this about? It was an ambush but those felt like low-rent mercenaries, not power-enhanced wizards. What am I missing here?

She spun when she sensed magic. A shimmering image of a beautiful silver-haired, silver-eyed woman in a trench coat and gloves appeared. Alison didn't recognize her, but given what Vincent had said, she assumed she was the Ultimate dealer.

Dad didn't eradicate all the Ultimate, but stopping the dealer at least stopped the flow in a city. That doesn't sound like a bad idea now.

"Good morning, Alison." The woman raised a gloved hand, her eyes mournful. "More mercenaries are now surrounding your employees as they rush toward the house, and a battle has begun. I presume by now that you realize you were not attacked by our true people. We anticipated you would try something, and we took measures to ensure that you would have to face us alone."

"Who are you?" she demanded. "If you're Tapestry and this is an attempt to goad me into giving you Omni, it won't work. You'll merely lose even more Strands. I'm very angry about the terrorist threat."

The woman sighed. "It doesn't matter who I am or even who I serve. What matters is that you have ten minutes to travel to the park at the following address." She stated it calmly with no inflection in her tone. "You'll find it's too far away for you to get there in time traveling by car. You'll be forced to travel there alone with your wings."

She shrugged. "And what if I simply say screw it and don't come? Maybe I'm tired of games."

Her adversary shook her head. "Then I'll have to go into the hospital across from the park and make an example of people. I don't want to have to do that, but I will. It's an easy environment to kill people if one is so inclined."

"How do I know you're not bluffing?" she countered. She found it hard to believe that the woman could be that ruthless.

"You don't know if I'm bluffing, but taking that chance is gambling with the lives of many people who are already vulnerable. I don't intend to debate this with you, Alison. The clock starts now. Make your choice." Her image disappeared.

Alison barreled out the cracked front doorway. A burst from a rifle narrowly missed her head. The mercenary was crouched near a small bush in the front, but his cover didn't protect him when she tossed a shadow crescent. It cut through the shrub and into the man. He cried out before he collapsed and blood gushed from the wound.

These guys don't even have deflectors. They relied too much on surprise. So this was nothing more than a distraction and maybe the vague hope they'd win?

Dark wings expanded from her back, and she ascended. A few other mercenaries appeared from the back of the house, fired, and narrowly missed her. She returned fire with light bolts and forced them to retreat behind the building.

She increased altitude. Her phone rang and the ring tone indicated that it was Tahir.

Quickly, she pulled it out and answered it. "Let the team know I'm on my way to a new location to save potential civilians, but they should clean up the mess I left behind. Keep your drone here to help them identify the stragglers, as there are several mercenaries still at the house in addition to the ones in the street."

"Are you sure you don't want to wait for backup?" he asked.

"We don't have time."

"Very well. I hope you know what you're doing, Alison."

"Probably not, but I'm off to stop our Ultimate dealer." She poured more magic into her wings and increased her flight speed. The first address might have been nothing more than an attempt to remove her reinforcements, but the enemy had made a critical mistake in showing their face. If she hadn't, Alison might not have been convinced she needed to go. Knowing this was the dealer made all the difference, and she was reasonably sure the woman was unaware that she had been described, even if only vaguely. She would need to thank Vincent later for his valuable intel.

CHAPTER TWENTY-TWO

She approached the park like an angry bat that had taken a wrong turn the previous night. Alison remained low to the ground. The scarcity of cars on the road and people outside kept her focused on the coming fight despite the sobering realization that if she hadn't taken Vincent's warning seriously, too many people might have ended up dead.

Brownstone Effect? Ha! It'll only be a Brownstone Effect when I don't have to worry about this kind of crap ever again.

After a few minutes of travel, she located the tall silhouette of the hospital the woman mentioned, which immediately raised doubts about whether the silver-haired woman had been bluffing.

If I'd refused, I'd still be here later and with more innocent people hurt. I need these people to pay. They think they can get away with that, but I need to make them understand that they can't.

She increased altitude to gain a better view of the sprawling, tree-filled park. The playgrounds and extensive jogging pathways lay empty, with only a single person near the center. It was the silver-haired woman in the trench coat. She sat on the edge of an empty fountain that had been drained for the winter and her hair fluttered in the wind.

This will work. This will work nicely.

Alison landed lightly about ten yards away from her opponent but not before she'd refreshed her shields and summoned a shadow blade. She retained her wings.

Magic radiated from the trees on all sides. Even if she couldn't see anything, the silver-haired woman wasn't alone.

The dealer's placid expression could have been borrowed from someone meditating in a yoga studio. The next minutes would determine if that was resignation or arrogance.

"I'm here," Alison called. "I'm almost insulted at what you tried earlier, and I'm definitely insulted by you threatening a hospital. That's not the way to last long in this city."

"I understand what it must seem like to you. More like the actions of cowardly vermin."

"That's one way of putting it."

The woman stood and shook her head. "I did what I needed to get you here alone."

She chuckled. "Which means you don't think you can win against me and all my people, let alone against me and my people and the cops. That doesn't exactly radiate confidence."

"I'm Mirela," the woman announced. "Please note that a few of my hirelings are launching diversionary attacks around town to occupy the law enforcement resources. If you expect reinforcements, they won't be coming."

Alison glared at her. "You bitch. You said if I came no one would get hurt."

"And I doubt anyone will. If they follow the plan, they will fire a few bullets and flee. If it makes you feel any better, they are mercenaries and merely interested in making a quick dollar, rather than dedicated ideologues or terrorists. I've told them I didn't want them to hurt anyone, and they have no reason to actually try to hurt anyone."

"So it was a lie, then? The hospital, too?"

Maybe I can get through to her if she's not a total psycho.

Mirela shook her head. "No. I intended to start on the first floor and slaughter people room by room until you came. Given everything I know about you, I suspect it wouldn't have taken long."

Alison blinked. The woman's tone was so matter of fact it was hard to believe she wasn't joking.

"Those people did nothing to you," she shouted.

"No, they didn't." The woman sighed. "Such is the injustice of this world. Please don't misinterpret me, Alison. I know what I intended was wrong, and I know much of what I have done is wrong, vicious, and cruel. I could spend time justifying my actions by speaking of targeting certain types of people—of vermin—but I know that's misleading. I have no illusions about what I am."

"And what is that?"

The dealer removed her gloves to reveal her crystal-covered hands before she unbelted her coat and shrugged it off, letting it pool at her feet. She wore no clothes except for her boots, perhaps because the rest of her body was covered with thick layers of jagged and uneven silver crystals. Her face shimmered for a moment, and the beautiful visage vanished and was replaced by small uneven mounds and patches of crystal. Her silver eyes turned black. The vague shape of a human woman was there, but the varied patterns and densities of the hard material on her skin often left them looking more like growths than a separate layer.

"I'm a monster, Alison," she explained.

Alison narrowed her eyes. "Ultimate changed you?"

She nodded. "Ultimate freed me to reach my maximum potential, and that was as a monster. It's how I best serve this world."

"So what? You want to turn everyone into a monster? Is that the Tapestry's plan?"

Mirela shook her head. "I wish to serve and facilitate something greater, and I don't serve the Tapestry." A hint of disdain flavored her words.

"But you know who they are?" she insisted. "Did they give you the True Cores?"

The woman squatted and reached into her trench coat. She withdrew a white True Core—a color Alison hadn't seen before—and held it out in her palm. "I know this seems insincere considering I'm probably about to kill you, but I do greatly admire you."

"Yeah, the whole killing me thing does kind of put a damper on that." She continued to watch her opponent even though she also tried to pay attention to the subtle shifts in magic on her flanks. "And all the people who targeted me before."

"I didn't tell those people to attack you. I warned

against it in several cases." Mirela sighed. "If they were more stable, perhaps things wouldn't have come to this, but such is our situation. Ultimate is more important than you could possibly understand for the future."

Alison shook her head. "You don't sound like the total psychos I dealt with before. You don't have to do this. I don't want to have to kill you. If this is about being transformed, I'm sure with some help, your transformation can be reversed."

"Reversed?" The dealer laughed. "Why would I want that? Haven't you listened to me?"

"No offense, but have you looked at yourself in a mirror?" she asked. "I'm not saying everyone has to be all smooth and I'm sure you'd be a big hit with the Harrikens, but people aren't supposed to be covered with crystals."

"One's appearance is irrelevant," the woman explained. "The change has given me power."

"And you'll use that to rule over others or some nonsense?"

"No, I'll use it to prove that I exist." Mirela scoffed. "You, of all people, should understand that. You don't seek to rule this city, but it swirls around you because of your power."

Alison shrugged. "You have a point, but I'm not the one who just threatened a *hospital*. Worth isn't about power. It's about how you wield it. I'll give you one last chance to surrender."

"I can agree with you on that. I'll give *you* one chance, but only because I respect you for what you've done against dark wizards and their foolish, exclusionary ways." The dealer nodded at the True Core. "Take it. Prove you're willing to join us. Embrace the future. Otherwise, you will die here and the plan will still proceed, but there will be one less useful person in this broken world."

"I'll have to go with a big no there." Her gaze cut to the left. She sensed magic near a couple of maple trees. "I don't care what Dust-addled plan you have devised or about your justifications. All I need to know is that your plans involve eating dangerous magical crystals that alternate between mutating people and making them crazy and also involves blood from magicals. Oh, and this whole plan is somehow at least indirectly linked to a group of creepy weirdos who have already tried to kill me and my friends for probably similar messed-up reasons."

Mirela shook her head and tossed the True Core on top of her coat. "Unfortunate. Kill her."

Alison launched upward and to her left and swung her sword. A black-veined wizard, suddenly visible, opened his mouth in surprise before she severed his head. Three other wizards and two witches, all black-eyed and dark veined, winked into existence.

They held their hands up and a surge of bright red, blue, and green orbs careened toward her. She circled a nearby tree. The missiles exploded against the trunk. Large chunks fell and the wounded tree cracked and split, which toppled the bulk of it to pound into the moist ground.

Her first retaliation was a light bolt fired into one of the witches. The enemy's shield absorbed the attack with ease and barely flickered. Her follow-up shadow crescent struck the same shield and dissipated in an instant.

Mirela raised both her arms above her head. She began to murmur in rapid Enochian. Complex sigils inscribed themselves in cerulean fire above her. They began to form nested layers, and the patterns increased in complexity.

Alison turned to fire at her but another barrage from the other magicals struck her. Two orbs exploded against her shield and hurled her into the branches of a tree. She righted herself and swooped toward the ground while her opponents shredded the tree and nearby ground with their explosive attacks. She pulled up at the last moment to avoid another direct strike.

These guys are tougher than I thought they'd be. I wonder if that has something to do with the white crystal.

Another blast impacted with her side. She hissed as she moved deeper into the forest and turned, her side stinging.

They're hitting me hard even with my shields. Damn. They're on a different level than the last few Ultimate users I fought.

Alison ascended quickly. Branches whipped her but bounced off her shield. Tree limbs exploded in showers of burning, smoking wood under the assault of her enemies. She fed more energy into her wings and shields as she broke free of the tree line. Several attacks streamed past her. She continued to climb, then put her hands together to feed her own orb—a growing, crackling ball of white flowing into cerulean light.

Mental note. Write a big check to the city later.

Another enemy orb caught her and she almost lost control of her spell, but she ignored the pain as she rose even higher and continued to gather her energy. She needed more time but blinding light bathed Mirela below.

I don't have time to stall. If she gets mad, she'll nuke the hospital.

She shunted most of her shield energy in front of her,

spun, and turned to dive directly toward the dealer. Her own orb had grown past the size of a large beach ball and the magical pressure was now difficult to contain. A steady stream of attacks rocketed around her like anti-aircraft artillery during the Blitz. She yelled as she zoomed closer and closer to her target.

When she was fifty feet away, she released the energy and her massive orb hurtled away from her hands. She twisted and let her momentum help carry her forward. Her wings now only maintained her height as she focused on strengthening her shield.

Her attack struck the ground with a resounding and deafening boom. A massive blue-white explosion erupted from the point of impact and grew like a tree under rapid time-lapse photography. The shockwave swept in all directions to obliterate the closest trees and fell others. The edge of her own attack caught her and she spiraled downward. She thumped into the moist dirt with a loud grunt and rolled several times, her shield depleted and deep burns on the side of her arm.

The cloud of flame and debris continued to climb into the sky, almost hypnotic before it began to fall back to Earth and left the air thick with heat and ash.

Alison groaned and stood, clutching her arm. She brushed ash off her face and took a few deep breaths before she murmured the healing spell that shrank her burns to nothing. Quickly, she summoned a new shield and extended her blade. Mirela couldn't have survived being at the epicenter, but some of her friends might have.

She advanced slowly and her gaze traversed the area constantly as the dust began to clear. The explosion had left a massive crater in the center of the park. The scorched remains of five bodies in the hole marked the final moments on Earth of the Ultimate users, but something else caught her attention.

"You have to be kidding me!" she shouted.

Mirela stumbled forward. Black blood dripped from wounds all over her body through jagged cracks in the crystal. This suggested that she wasn't a woman with a crystal skin but a woman composed of layer upon layer of the same material. For a brief moment, Alison could even see a beating crystal heart covered in black. Besides the cracks, light shined through several large holes in body, legs, and even her head.

"You should have used that attack before I had time to channel any power, Alison," her adversary called. She raised her arm and put her fingers together. "I must admit, I didn't think you would go so far." The cracks and holes began to seal and new crystals grew in to fill the missing mass. "But that proves this plan is worth it. Even the great Alison Brownstone had to go all out to stop me. I should have simply killed you when you arrived, but I wanted to prove the power of Ultimate, and I maintained some vague hope of persuading you to join us."

Alison raised her arms and gritted her teeth. If explosives didn't work, it was time for a different strategy. A brilliant lance of energy winked into existence in front of her and lines of shadow danced across its length. She ignored the woman and the strain of her magic use as she poured energy into it.

The dealer dropped to all fours and loped toward her

with sudden speed, her limbs rotating at inhuman angles. "You will not win!"

She narrowed her eyes and continued to feed the spell. Her enemy closed in seconds and leapt toward her with a crystal-covered hand poised to strike.

"I'm sorry," she said and released her spell.

The digging lance bored into Mirela's chest with a deep thrum. The weapon spun once it made contact with the woman. A sickening crunching and cracking filled the air, along with a flurry of sparks as it drilled through her chest and hurled the dealer back a good ten yards before it finally dissipated.

Mirela fell with most of her body now missing. Alison summoned a shadow blade and rushed forward, ready to deal the fatal blow. She slowed to a stop. No new crystals grew in the vast emptiness that had once been the woman's chest.

"You left me no choice," she murmured and lowered her sword.

A hollow gasp escaped the wounded dealer. "Alphonse, forgive me."

Alison shook her head.

What a waste.

She retrieved her phone and dialed Tahir. "What's the situation?"

"Hana, Drysi, and Mason have neutralized all the mercs in the neighborhood. They have almost immobilized all the survivors and are waiting for the police to arrive. There also were multiple simultaneous attacks in the city as well, but the police and PDA quickly neutralized those forces."

"Those were only distractions," she replied. "I'll explain to everyone in detail. Do you have eyes on me yet?"

"I have eyes on a massive smoking crater," he commented, a hint of disapproval in his voice. "And you. Did you handle all of them?"

"Yeah." She sighed. "I couldn't take any of them alive, but I did find out that our silver-haired friend wasn't the mastermind behind Ultimate."

"Who is then?" he asked.

"Alphonse Tatum," she stated. "I guess Vincent was right. I'll wait until the cops get here." She looked at the crater. "This has been a crazy February."

CHAPTER TWENTY-THREE

"You can't do this," Alphonse shouted and his hands twitched. "Don't you fools understand? I know independent thought is probably forbidden in your little group, but try to think for a second before you act."

A plain brown-haired man in a suit tilted his head slightly from across the otherwise dusty, empty room. He was the main Weaver he had dealt with thus far—as far as he knew, at least. He really did have a hard time telling members of the Tapestry apart and assumed they used magic to adopt a similar appearance once they joined the group.

Much of their inner workings and goals remained mysterious to him, but he hadn't honestly cared as long as they supplied him with the materials he needed for his experiments, from more basic potion reagents to the True Cores. The nature of the Cores still eluded him as well, with his current theory being that they represented some kind of concentrated magical essence from a powerful Oriceran creature. Additional investigation into the Cores would follow his other research, but neither could occur if the Tapestry cut him off as they now threatened to do.

"Why can't we do it?" the Weaver asked. "I do not understand."

He jabbed his finger in the air. "My experiments can't proceed in their current form without True Cores. They are the cornerstone of my research. You understood that before. It's why you agreed to give them to me and now, you're saying we're done. It's absurd. I've made so much progress in a short time—far more than I suspect you have. How long has your group had access to the Cores? Months? Years? Centuries? There's a reason you needed outside help."

The Weaver stared at him with no emotion on his face. There was something inordinately frustrating about losing an argument with a man who genuinely didn't seem to care. He prided himself on his emotional control, but his losses that week had been staggering. His best experiments had all perished thanks to Brownstone's meddling. He alternated between being disappointed that he'd lost such a stable experiment as Mirela and agitated by the failure of her plan.

"The True Cores are something we have provided," the Weaver continued. "In every instance when they have been given to you, that has occurred because of a possibility that the research would benefit the Tapestry. We care little about your research other than in that regard. We also care little if you have wasted time. It is your time to waste. The True Cores are not your property nor are you entitled to them." His tone remained flat and lifeless. "Any appeals based on emotion or how they affect you and your plans will not be effective. We would suggest you not continue with such a strategy as it is a waste of our mutual time."

"You don't understand. I'm so close now. Far closer than I've ever been." Alphonse shook his head. "Don't you see? Even the battle was proof of that. Alison Brownstone basically had to destroy a park to win against one of my experiments. She is a Drow princess and one of the most powerful magicals in the country, and I was able to almost match her with enhancements to source material who had almost no magic. Can't you get it through your pathetic little head? We're talking about producing Alison Brownstone-level power on command. What if every Strand had that power?"

The wizard had never intended to give the Tapestry the power, but he hoped they believed enough in the concept to support the research until he had fully mastered it. He refused to believe that excessive mutations were necessary, but he was willing to ignore that if the path forward left him no choice.

The Weaver shook his head. "Your so-called powerful experiments lost against one woman. That in and of itself isn't something of strong consideration in our final decision given her relative power, as you have noted. But to produce those experiments, we have had to provide considerable resources that are not easy to obtain on Earth. Our analyses indicate there is a low probability of you being able to produce anyone as strong as Mirela again, let alone anyone stronger. Simple cost-benefit analysis suggests, therefore, that supporting your research is no longer to our benefit and is, in fact, a waste of resources."

JUDITH BERENS

"You don't know anything. You lack insight. You lack genius." He scoffed. "This is why you came to me for help. I can produce better results than you can, and you know it because you lack any spark of creativity in your little cult. If you stop supplying me now, what will you have gained? Nothing. But if you continue to provide me with True Cores, I'm confident I can achieve my desired results within months."

"Firstly, engaging in a sunk cost fallacy does not mean we would achieve useful management of our limited resources," the Weaver replied. "Secondly, with regard to you achieving your desired results within months, that seems unlikely given the current conditions in this area. Local law enforcement, federal law enforcement, local criminal organizations, and local bounty hunting organizations, along with Brownstone Security, are now all cognizant of the particular risk of Ultimate and are seeking you. Our analyses indicate that Seattle is no longer a viable testing ground for experiments centered around Ultimate. We will not change our decision in this regard. You have had your chance to prove your theories here already."

Alphonse frowned before he took a deep breath and nodded. He could still salvage the situation in a different way. "I understand, but that doesn't mean there are no other places where we can test Ultimate, especially in different forms. There are thousands of cities in the world. Yes, Seattle has some unique properties that make it interesting and useful for my research, but it is far from being the only place that might suit the needs of the project. If this city is compromised by Brownstone's presence, I'll simply go somewhere else. The research cannot stop, no matter what."

"The needs of your project pale before the needs of the Tapestry." The colorless tone seemed far more insulting and threatening than real emotion would have been. "This entire Ultimate research endeavor has depleted us of limited and valuable resources for a net loss. It is the belief of the Overseer that support of the project is no longer justified, regardless of location. The probability of a success useful to our overall plans is too low to justify outlays of resources."

The wizard snorted and his hand inched toward one of his pockets. If the Tapestry was done with his research, he also suspected they were done with him. "So that's it? You've decided it's done? After everything I've achieved and despite everything we could achieve together? Myopic doesn't even begin to describe it."

"Yes, Alphonse Tatum. That is what has been decided. Your usefulness to the Tapestry is at an end. You are free to consider it myopia if you will, but you will be dead soon. We will use your body for our own purposes. You will join with the Tapestry."

The door opened and five Strands entered. All wore the blandest expression possible for executioners.

He chuckled and fingered a vial in his pocket. "Do you know why I'm vastly superior to everyone in your little cult, including the Overseer?"

The Weaver shook his head. "But you are not superior. You cannot exceed the Tapestry. You are an individual. We are the Tapestry."

"But I am superior, and I can prove it."

"Intriguing. How would you prove this? What metrics would you use?"

"I don't need to use any special metrics." He used his thumb to pop the lid of the potion still in his pocket. "You've already proven it with your own statements. Because you eschew individuality. You're so focused on being nothing more than a piece of a greater whole that you forget the best way to accomplish that is by being the greatest individual."

"Do not worry, Alphonse Tatum. You will soon be made useful." The Weaver nodded at the Strands. "Minimize damage to the body. We will proceed with processing within an hour."

"Amateurs," the wizard sneered.

"There is no such concept among the Tapestry."

The five Strands marched forward, their hands outstretched.

Alphonse yanked the potion out of his pocket and swung his arm in a wide arc. A small amount of the ochre liquid inside splashed on the approaching Strands. The liquid sizzled when it touched the men and a moment later, greens flame erupted around them. They collapsed with grunts but none screamed, even while they burned to death.

"You're no better than anyone else." He grinned. "Everyone always underestimates potion wizards." He hurled the container toward the Weaver. It shattered against the man and released the small amount of remaining liquid. Seconds later, his opponent lay on the floor and burned alive, as eerily quiet as his comrades had been.

The wizard clucked his tongue and retrieved a few more potions. The Tapestry would pay for their disrespect. He strolled out of the room and into the dusty great room at the front of the building. A dozen Strands looked at him, cocked their hands, and attacked.

He snorted and threw a magic concoction into the center of the group. The glass vial landed with a thud and exploded in a puff of purple smoke. Thick, barbed vines erupted from the smoke and impaled the Strands in under a second. He folded his arms and tapped his foot until every man lay impaled and twitched as their blood dripped on the floor.

He whistled and headed to the front door. When he opened it, he was unsurprised to see a few more Strands waiting. His next potion exploded in the middle of the group and scattered them across the barren lawn of the abandoned mansion.

Alphonse looked over his shoulder and shook his head. He retrieved another vial and threw it hard against the wall. The glass splintered, and the dark oily liquid slid down the side for a few seconds before it burst into flames. Within ten seconds, fire licked hungrily at the building.

"Ah, Mirela, it's unfortunate that I lost you, but you were such a useful experiment. It'll take me some time to find as useful a reagent as a True Core. This has been a hard week, indeed."

The wizard withdrew another potion and looked around. He didn't see any living Strands and the fire was spreading. He might need to avoid Seattle for a few months, but he suspected Alison Brownstone would clean up the Tapestry for him and then, it wouldn't matter. He continued toward his rental Mazda, a dull gray model. Sometimes, it helped to not stand out. He could appreciate that aspect of the Tapestry.

A suited man stepped out of the bushes with the standard plain brown hair and an easy to forget face. Another Strand.

Alphonse sighed. "Please don't make me waste a potion on a single Strand. You're not worth it, especially with the quality of the potions I've used."

"We are not a Strand," the man related, his voice as lifeless as any of the other Tapestry members. "Probability analysis suggested the possibility that you would escape your execution."

"Congratulations on your successful deduction. Am I supposed to be impressed?" He tucked his potion into his pocket and pulled his wand out. Having to rely on direct spells always felt like an admission of vulgar technique. He pointed his wand at the man. "This is the Tapestry's fault. You fools shouldn't have attempted to double-cross me."

"We stand by our execution decision, and there was a high probability that you would betray us."

"You're fools. You could have had so much if only you'd trusted my research. Goodbye, Strand. Better luck in your next life."

He chanted a rapid fireball spell. A bright orange-red orb launched from the tip of the wand and barreled toward his adversary. It impacted with an invisible shield and the blast shunted off to either side. The Strand remained untouched and his expression unchanged.

"Oh, you have a few tricks, do you?" He tucked his wand away and yanked out another potion. "Maybe you are worth this, then." He hurled it, and the force of the bright white explosion even knocked him onto his butt. The hard landing hurt somewhat, but he looked across at his adversary with a grin.

When the smoke cleared, the target still stood although the front of his suit and body was blackened and charred.

The burned man opened his cracked mouth. "We are the Overseer. Your treachery was foreseen, Alphonse Tatum, as were your methods of escape. You represent a risk to the Tapestry. You would bring Alison Brownstone or other enemies upon us and so cannot be allowed to live. You must understand that you would never be allowed to escape."

Alphonse glared at the Overseer. "You don't look any different than the rest."

His adversary strolled toward him. A fleshy, barbed tentacle burst from his side and ripped through his suit.

"What in the name of the two worlds are you?" the wizard whispered.

"We are the Tapestry."

The tentacle pierced his heart.

CHAPTER TWENTY-FOUR

Alison wiggled her butt a little in her chair. She doubted she could be more comfortable without a spell. "This is very comfortable, Agent Latherby. You didn't even have chairs for the longest time in your office, and now you have new, fancy chairs? You're in serious danger of developing a personality." She bounced a few times. "I think I'll have to get this for my office."

"I'll send you the catalog number." The PDA agent chuckled. "I've seen the wisdom of making sure certain guests are comfortable, especially when they've provided as much aid to the PDA and the city as you have. You've spent enough time in this office to earn your own chair."

"I don't suppose that aid includes helping me pay for the damage to the park?" She offered an apologetic smile.

"Unfortunately not. The mayor, PDA, and police are very understanding, but still..." He shook his head. "Think of it this way. You don't have to pay for new buildings, only groundskeeping and planting—and that's one of the reasons I wanted to talk to you today, actually."

"You want to talk about me blowing parks up?" She sighed. "I honestly did what I thought I needed to do to win the fight. My choices were either kill her, let her kill me, or have her attack a hospital. Or have you found some haunted park you need me to obliterate?" She gave him a sheepish grin.

"No one is contesting your use of force against the enemy in the park. Let me be clear about that." Agent Latherby frowned and leaned forward. "This concerns the information you passed on about Mirela—whom we have identified as one Mirela Lilova—and her last words."

"Alphonse Tatum," Alison declared. She gritted her teeth. "Please tell me you caught him. That guy's now linked to two major things that could have screwed this city over. He's a menace, and even the last thing he helped with would be enough to have him locked up in an Ultramax."

"Oh, the PDA, FBI, DEA, and a number of other agencies all agree with that assessment, but it's irrelevant at this juncture so I wouldn't spend too much worrying about it."

She frowned. "Don't tell me you found him and you're letting him go in exchange for information or something? If that's your call, fine, but I can't let him go. He'll end up destroying a city when he gets bored."

He shook his head. "No, this is a more direct, practical issue, not a legal one. The Seattle police found his body floating in the bay the other day. He's dead. Quite thoroughly and completely, I'm happy to say. Someone had ripped his heart out, but there's still some confusion about the exact nature of what or who attacked him. Given this city, it could be almost anything."

Alison scrubbed a hand down her face and blew a breath out. "Was a magical examination performed?"

"Yes, and it didn't turn up much other than verifying that he died from the rather obvious and apparent injury."

"What? Are you telling me someone might poison someone and then rip their heart to cover it up?"

Agent Latherby shrugged. "I've seen similar things in my career."

"Huh. Okay. They have absolutely no evidence that might indicate what it is?"

"There are traces of cellular residue from an unidentified organism, but that description applies to large numbers of the creatures on Oriceran, so it's hard to learn anything useful with that particular information. But we and the police have different people looking into it. If there's something to find, we'll find it."

"So his heart was torn out?" She pondered the gory demise and made a face. "Given what I saw from some of the Ultimate users, I wouldn't be surprised if it was one of them. Maybe, unlike Mirela, someone didn't like what they became and decided to get a little revenge. It'd be a nice and poetic end for a monster who didn't look like one."

"It is a strong possibility, among others. In a sense, although this cuts off certain avenues of investigation, his death does free up agency resources that we had devoted to the search for him, and it also does seem to suggest Ultimate is over." Agent Latherby withdrew his tablet from a drawer and tapped on it a few times. He turned it to face her. It depicted a map of the US with red dots in various places.

"What's this?" Alison asked. There was no header or legend to clarify things.

"These mark incidents believed to be associated with Ultimate in one form or another. It's all based on local police self-reporting. This represents all of February." The agent gestured to Texas, Colorado, and Washington, which all contained several dots. A few others were sprinkled around the country and Canada. He swiped on the image, and a new map appeared. Only a tiny handful of dots remained, and all were in Texas. "With Lilova and Tatum killed, there doesn't appear to be continued, sustained dealing of Ultimate. As rare as this situation is, it does appear that this all comes down to a single man and his core of assistants. A scourge has been removed from the country. The fact that Ultimate incidents continue to decline strongly suggests Tatum wasn't killed by a rival dealer or user."

"Ultimate might be done for now, but the Tapestry is still out there. Based on what I saw and what that woman told me, they were the suppliers of the True Cores. I don't know if Tatum did something to the True Cores, but the fact that they are involved in changing people should mean that everyone has a little more trouble sleeping at night. Ultimate might return. The quicker we find the Tapestry, the less chance there is of that returning."

"I'm not inclined to disagree, but unfortunately, with Tatum and his people dead—even if they were linked to the Tapestry—we no longer have any viable leads. That aside, if they were the supplier of some of the ingredients, the fact that Ultimate is disappearing indicates that Tatum's expertise was likely required for at least some key aspect."

Agent Latherby nodded at the tablet. "We might not have won the war, but we've won the battle. You should be proud of your successes. Both you and your father played key roles in stopping a dangerous drug from spreading across the country to perhaps the world."

"The world? Do you think so?" She frowned.

He nodded. "It's our belief that they were simply refining it before mass production. Your father and his men encountered the more basic version, and you encountered the more refined version. Whether they call it pure or whatnot is irrelevant. It was merely a matter of time before they finished their modifications and began to pump it everywhere. Imagine all the chaos of rogue magicals we already have to deal with, except with considerably more power and fewer restrictions." He scoffed. "Your father would have to come out of retirement."

"That would make him and my mom grumpy, and trust me, you don't want two Brownstones grumpy. I don't know if the world could survive." Alison managed a smile. "A win, huh? I can live with that, and the Tapestry will hopefully lie low for a while. For all I know, they're still recruiting new guys. They lost a ton of men when we last fought them."

"The government's keeping an eye out for them," the agent confirmed. "We don't have enough official evidence for an organizational bounty, but I'm sure that will come sooner rather than later. Hopefully, they'll be a distant memory before long, exactly like the Seventh Order."

She grinned. "A girl can dream."

"It's very hard to take you seriously when you have a squirrel on your head." Alison laughed.

Hana leaned against a wall, her arms folded. Omni perched atop her head in his latest form. "I taught him this trick. It impresses people." She held her hand out, and the squirrel scampered into it. When she set him gently on the floor, he hurried over to a bowl of seeds to munch away. "And he's well-behaved up there, so I'm never worried. It kind of started when he was in bird form, and we simply took it to his other forms. He doesn't turn into anything super-creepy, so it's not a problem."

She's so happy, but I need to keep things real.

"It's not over with the Tapestry yet." She shrugged. "I wanted to make that clear to you, but everything else will stay the same. The pet park will open here soon, and we'll keep Omni here during the day. But all we did was mess up a side business for the Tapestry, not the main mission, whatever the hell that is. I'm still sure that head-riding squirrel is at the heart of it, though."

Her friend shrugged. "I don't really mind or care. The way I see it, the future's not real, so why should I even worry about it?"

"The future's not real?" Alison quirked a brow. "What makes you say that? What happens after today?"

"More today. Once the future comes, it's simply the present, right?" She grinned. "So the only thing you should worry about—I mean *really* worry about—is the present, and that's what I've decided to think about it."

"I'm not sure I agree with that, but I can see where you're coming from." She knelt beside Omni and scratched his neck. "You're really not worried? I suppose I can worry enough for the both of us."

"No, I'm not worried. Why should I worry? Because they almost killed me?" The fox blew a raspberry. "They *almost* killed me, but we actually killed tons of them, and if they come back, my little fur-scale-feather baby will shred them into kibble and have them for lunch. Nope, as far as I'm concerned, the Tapestry is zero for two, and you know what happens when you go up for that third strike?"

"You're out." Alison grinned.

Hana winked. "Exactly."

CHAPTER TWENTY-FIVE

Alison yawned as she crested the stairs and padded toward her bedroom in her pajamas. She turned at a creak behind her. Sonya stepped out of her room. The teen looked at her, snorted, and stepped back into her room.

With a heavy sigh, she entered her bedroom. Things had been tense with Sonya since the showdown with Mirela.

Mason lay on the bed and thumbed images on his phone. He looked up. "Let me guess, Sonya's still mad at you? Sometimes, I can't tell because it's like she's being extra sweet to me to make up for it."

"I never thought letting a teenager sleep in would piss her off so much." She shrugged, headed over to the bed, and lay down beside him. "I thought I was doing her a favor that morning."

"You have to remember that she's in an awkward place. She's a young teenager, but she also works as a professional infomancer and she idolizes you, A." He set his phone down. "You should try to understand what it looks like from her perspective. Basically, to her, both her idol and boss benched her during an important mission because she's young. She thinks you don't believe in her ability and that she couldn't contribute to the mission."

Alison groaned. "I told her that's not what it was about, and she's helped on many important missions. She helped defend the building when it was attacked."

Mason grinned. "Yes, because teenagers are always so logical. It's no big deal. You know her. She'll get over it. But don't let her sleep in next time, or you'll really have to suffer her wrath."

"You'd think I'd be halfway decent at understanding teenagers considering I was one not all that long ago." She shook her head. "And, sure, I went to magic school, but I still had a semi-normal teenage life with friends, classes, and—"

"Dragons?" he suggested. "And Louper?"

She mock-punched him in the arm. "The point is that it's not like it was with my mom. I didn't work a dangerous job as a teenager. I had the occasional dangerous adventure, but my life wasn't focused around that." She frowned at a sudden thought. "Mom would probably have some insight and advice, given her situation around that age. I should ask her."

He laughed. "She'll probably tell you that Sonya needs to learn how to kill people quicker, or at least how to cripple them more effectively."

"Probably. Either that or insist that I force her to study ancient history for the next year."

"True enough."

"I guess it's good training," Alison suggested. "All this stuff with Sonya, I mean."

Mason peered at her, a mischievous glint in his eye. "Good training for what, exactly?"

"You know...kids." She shrugged. "In the future. Not right now. I think at the minimum, I should at least eliminate the Tapestry and get Rasila and Miar under control before I consider having any kids. That's a little too many balls to juggle. My parents waited until they had things really quiet to have a kid, even if it was something of a surprise."

"Waiting sounds reasonable. And, sure, you probably shouldn't have kids before you've destroyed the Tapestry." He smirked. "I'm sure everyone always thinks about this kind of thing that way."

"I'm just saying." She sighed and rested her head on his shoulder. "Normal life? Even when I was young and not caught up in fighting weird groups with funny names, I wasn't normal. I could see people's souls, for crying out loud, and you're right. I went to a magic school to learn spells and hang out in the kemana. Is that normal or not normal? I honestly don't know anymore. We live in a world connected to a world of magic. Not all people might be magical, but it influences them every day."

"I think normal is relative." He stroked her hair. "I grew up in a family that expected me to be a healer of some kind, but I became a bodyguard and then a security contractor. Which is normal? I don't know either. I think there's no such thing as normal. There's only what works for you, and that's different for everyone."

Alison nodded. "I've chased it for too long, and it's messed me up. Normalcy, or at least what I thought it would be. I thought I wasn't doing that, but I realize I have. That even partially motivated why I moved to Seattle on some level." She sighed. "But I'm happy now, and part of that is because I'm leaving behind caring too much about what is normal. Don't get me wrong. I could do with a few fewer people like Alphonse Tatum in my life, but I have great friends, a great boyfriend, great parents, a great administrative assistant, and great people in general. All those greats are important. I also have strong magic powers, and I even have two Drow princesses to help take over from Myna. All in all, I have a great life, and I know I stress about things, but I also know I'm blessed in so many ways."

"I don't disagree, and I'm glad to hear you say it that way." Mason pulled her against his chest. "You know I think you're wonderful, A." He frowned. "And by the way, I let it go earlier because I wanted everything to settle down, but I don't know how much I appreciated it when you flew off to a secondary fight and left me behind. I can't have your back if I'm miles away."

"Sometimes, shit happens. You know how it goes, but it does make me think that once things have stabilized a little, we'll also look into hiring more magicals and doing more integration training with Jerry's group. Our teams are good and strong, but it wouldn't kill us to have two or three quality strong teams for situations like this. Sometimes, I feel like we are spread a little too thin."

He chuckled and ruffled her hair. "You don't want a security firm. You want an army. The Brownstone Army gets deployed to pacify the unruly Seattle rebels."

"I only want my city to be safe. I've accepted, like my dad did, that with power comes trouble, but I'm also trying to learn the same lesson he did." Alison shook her head. "When my dad met Trey, he was simply some punk gang member off the street with no magic. Now, Trey can regularly deal with a level-four on his own and has even done the occasional level-five. Being able to handle yourself isn't always about the power you were born with, and I need to keep that in mind when I deal with people, magical or otherwise."

"True enough." He stared at her, an almost unnervingly warm smile on his face.

"Why are you looking at me like that?"

"How should I look at you? Do you want me to scowl at you?"

"No, but it's kind of creeping me out." She shrugged. "It's like you have a secret that I don't know about. Everyone seems to have secrets around here except Hana. For a former con woman, she's remarkably open about everything. The rest of us keep dragging secrets of one form or another around."

"I don't have any secrets from you, not anymore." He shrugged. "I've told you everything. I haven't gone through every last girlfriend I've ever had, though, but we can if you want." He grinned.

She threw her hand up. "I don't need to hear it. You've told me enough."

"And you've told me everything, including the truth about your dad." Mason's expression turned serious. "And I think that's changed something important, and that's why I'm smiling like a creeper."

"What do you mean? Why do you think it changes anything?"

"It doesn't change it in a bad way," he replied. "But there's always been something there between us—a distance. I could feel it. I knew you were holding something back from me, and I couldn't help but wonder what it was. I love you, so I want to know everything about you, and it felt like you couldn't trust me. Now, of course, I realize you couldn't tell me because it wasn't your secret to tell."

Alison nodded. "And I told you guys all that stuff, but I was probably wrong."

He frowned in sudden confusion. "Wrong?"

"Yeah, about the Tapestry. I had convinced myself they are aliens, but after everything that happened this month, I'm convinced they're merely a weird group of wizards." She shrugged.

"Huh? Really? What brought you to that conclusion? I don't know either way, but I've dealt with fewer aliens than you have."

"Seeing and killing Mirela is what changed my mind," she murmured and the ghost of regret colored her words. "She'd been heavily changed, but she was still a human. Besides, why would aliens risk working with a dangerous rogue wizard?"

"I, for one, am glad you were wrong. It forced you to tell me about your dad and now, I don't have any more doubts. Not that I had many, to begin with."

She chuckled. "They never talk about how murderous wizards can help a relationship by encouraging honesty in any of the relationship books. I don't think my dad mentioned that from any of the relationship podcasts he used to listen to."

Mason laughed. "No, I don't think there is anything like that. Maybe we can write that book. *Men are from Earth and Women are from Oriceran.* It'll be a huge bestseller."

Alison gave him a mock-serious look. "Leave the security game and become authors? Maybe. I'll have to think about it."

He leaned over and opened the drawer on his nightstand. "So, I've been doing some thinking, A. I had thought about this before, but this month really brought it home, which is another reason why I was smiling."

"What were you thinking about?" She rolled the opposite way to get comfortable and yawned.

"Turn around, please, A." He coughed. "This is something I think you need to see."

She sat and turned toward him. He held a small black velvet box with a diamond ring nestled inside. She gasped and her eyes widened.

"Is…that…uh…"

Mason laughed. "Very articulate. Look, it's a nice ring, but it's not charged by the moon to generate magical force fields or anything like that, and the wedding ring won't have anything like that either. I really thought hard about whether you'd want or need something like that, but I think I know you well enough to know you don't. And I also know you won't want the wedding until at least after we've handled the Tapestry."

"Uh…" she whispered.

He slid out of the bed with the box and walked around to her side. "I've asked myself for weeks—if not months—

whether I needed some grand gesture, but I decided that it was only a way to stall. I know what I want, and I know who I want. I'm in love with you. We live together. We work together, and I have a hard time imagining a future without you in it." He dropped to one knee. "Alison Brownstone, will you marry me?"

Alison stared at the ring and her eyes glistened. She reached out and hesitated for a moment before she slipped the ring on. "Yes, Mason, I will marry you." She gasped and slapped a hand over her mouth as an almost-Hana-like attack of giggles overwhelmed her.

Mason blinked. "The yes part I like, but I'm not so sure about the giggling."

She bit her lip and wiped tears of both joy and mirth from her eyes. "Now that you know the truth about my dad, I can tell you the truth about how he proposed. That's what I'm laughing about. It's why I appreciate your *normal* way of proposing."

"How?" he asked, suspicion in his voice.

"Some Nine Systems Alliance asshole arrived in a spaceship and basically threatened to grab him and run him off to a space jail. Then, out of nowhere, the military appeared and said they'd annihilate anyone who kidnapped an American citizen." She laughed. "My mom wanted an epic proposal, and my dad thought, 'Aliens, spaceships, the Army. That's fucking epic.' So he did it. Oh, Senator Johnston was there, too."

Mason burst out laughing. "You're kidding."

She fell back into laughter. "No, it's totally the truth. Apparently, the alien was super-confused about what was going on."

They both spent a good thirty seconds laughing before they calmed and took deep breaths.

He rested his forehead against hers. "Thank you, Alison, for saying yes, even though I didn't have the Army, a senator, or an alien."

Alison kissed him lightly on the lips. "It's fine. All I really need is you."

The story is far from over. Alison and her team's adventure continues in <u>RISE UP.</u>

FREE BOOKS!

WARNING:
The Troll is now in charge.
And he's giving away free books
if you sign-up!

Join the only newsletter hosted by a Troll!

Get sneak peeks, exclusive giveaways, behind the scenes
content, and more.
PLUS you'll be notified of special **one day only fan
pricing** on new releases.

CLICK HERE

or visit: https://marthacarr.com/read-free-stories/

For Hire: Teachers for special school in Virginia countryside.

Must be able to handle teenagers with special abilities.

Cannot be afraid to discipline werewolves, wizards, elves and other assorted hormonal teens.

Apply at the School of Necessary Magic.

AVAILABLE AT AMAZON RETAILERS

THE PEABRAIN'S IDEA

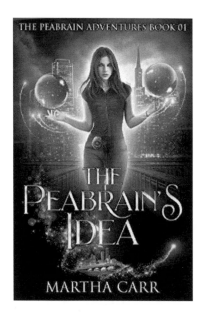

AVAILABLE ON AMAZON AND IN KINDLE UNLIMITED!

I have a terrible sense of direction. I like to think my inner compass is in there, but it's spinning in every direction. My favorite part is that I've been like this since I arrived on Earth and yet, when faced with two possibilities, I am once again convinced the direction I took was correct. It never is.

I walk down the street or take that turn with optimism, no thought of the million previous turns and slowly as the vista changes in ways I didn't expect I catch on once again. I'm going in the wrong direction.

I did it so often in Chicago and ended up continually in sketchy neighborhoods that the Offspring bought me an early form of those GPS things you hang in your car. He was tired of worrying about me. That thing was amazing, even if it still required a little common sense so I didn't end up turning into Lake Michigan. There was still that one time a new friend and I walked in the wrong direction till someone stopped us on the street as the sun went down and told us to call a taxi immediately heading the other way.

The stranger part is that I never worried, still don't. I marveled at the different scenery and worked out how to turn around and get back on the path I was meant to be on. It can even still happen on the highways of Texas with the multiple overpasses and necessary split-second decision. I can still test out my phone's ability to reroute, and occasionally I ignore it and try my methods. Once in a blue moon, I'm right and give myself way too much credit, but I still feel like a champion driving home.

Here's what I get out of this learning opportunity. We all have our strengths and the places we need help. The ability to ask for help and take it in and use it is priceless. It takes a lot of honesty and some healthy humility to admit what I can't do, or what's not working, and then to just take the assistance without adding my own two cents. Mostly, I do that to prove I know something – but is that really necessary or helpful? I'll tell you, in my case, that's a big no. In the meantime, if I can keep a sense of humor and enjoy the ride the journey will seem that much better – like a bonus just for me. More adventures to follow.

AUTHOR NOTES - MICHAEL ANDERLE

JULY 22, 2019

THANK YOU for not only reading this story but these *Author Notes* as well.

(I think I've been good with always opening with "thank you." If not, I need to edit the other *Author Notes*!)

RANDOM (*sometimes*) THOUGHTS?

I'm going to crib off of Martha's comments and discuss directions and not getting too upset with myself.

Generally, *I'm right.*

Ok, so I have to provide a bit more explanation with a healthy dose of caveats. If I know I'm wrong, I'll admit it (usually, sometimes I go down swinging 'cause of ego... I try to recognize those times.) If I know I'm right, I'll argue. If I think I'm right, I'll also argue (because my thinking makes me believe I'm right... See comment above.)

If I'm not sure, I'll actually say I don't know. I'd rather admit to not knowing than think I'm right and be proved wrong.

(Yes, I'll go secretly look up the data to make sure I was

wrong. It's a personality defect, I know.)

But, I won't argue for being right when I know I'm wrong.

So, all the time I'm right, I fight for it. When I think I'm right, I'll fight for those (and occasionally lose.)

When I don't know or suspect I'm wrong, I won't fight for it. So, I rarely 'lose' those arguments.

Therefore, generally I'm right. ;-)

At least, that's what my mind thinks is right.

AROUND THE WORLD IN 80 DAYS

One of the interesting (at least to me) aspects of my life is the ability to work from anywhere and at any time. In the future, I hope to re-read my own *Author Notes* and remember my life as a diary entry.

Riding in a Cadillac Escalade on the way to Los Angeles International Airport (LAX)

Interior is black leather, and there are free bottles of water waiting for Judith (my wife) and I to drink as we head down the 605 freeway. I'm tippity-typing as we move along to get these author notes out for tomorrows release of Alison Brownstone.

Did you enjoy it? Have you read about Daddy Brownstone yet? If not, we meet Alison in TUMB 01 (The Unbelievable Mr. Brownstone book 01) and she changes a man's life all around.

Kind of like she does in these stories (well, for the better anyway - she doesn't always change lives for the better in these books.)

I'm embarking on a five (5) week trip around the world for our publishing business. We start by sharing skills and thoughts with a bunch of authors in Edinburgh, Scotland. Then move down to Germany and will meet with business partners for audiobook distribution in Germany.

After some research, we end up in Dublin Ireland for World-Con and once that event is finished, we fly to Beijing, China for the Beijing Book Fair.

Finally, we fly to LAX and the trip will have gone 'round the world'.

It was never on my bucket-list to travel around the world, but you can bet I'm penciling in the effort so I can check it off.

Thank you to all of the readers of our books, allowing us to accomplish goals we didn't know we might have!

FAN PRICING

$0.99 Saturdays (new LMBPN stuff) and $0.99 Wednesday (both LMBPN books and friends of LMBPN books.) Get great stuff from us and others at tantalizing prices.

Go ahead, I bet you can't read just one.

Sign up here: http://lmbpn.com/email/.

HOW TO MARKET FOR BOOKS YOU LOVE

Review them so others have your thoughts, tell friends and the dogs of your enemies (because who wants to talk with enemies?)... *Enough said ;-)*

Ad Aeternitatem,

Michael Anderle

OTHER SERIES IN THE ORICERAN
UNIVERSE:

SCHOOL OF NECESSARY MAGIC
SCHOOL OF NECESSARY MAGIC: RAINE CAMPBELL
ALISON BROWNSTONE
THE DANIEL CODEX SERIES
THE LEIRA CHRONICLES
I FEAR NO EVIL
FEDERAL AGENTS OF MAGIC
THE UNBELIEVABLE MR. BROWNSTONE
REWRITING JUSTICE
THE KACY CHRONICLES
MIDWEST MAGIC CHRONICLES
SOUL STONE MAGE
THE FAIRHAVEN CHRONICLES

OTHER BOOKS BY JUDITH BERENS

OTHER BOOKS BY MARTHA CARR

JOIN THE ORICERAN UNIVERSE FAN GROUP ON FACEBOOK!

Made in the USA
Middletown, DE
12 December 2021

55301130R00149